A King Production presents…

All I See Is The Money…

Female Hustler 4

A Novel

JOY DEJA KING

Cover concept by Joy Deja King
Cover model: Joy Deja King
Editor: Jacqueline Ruiz: tinx518@aol.com
Library of Congress Cataloging-in-Publication Data;

A King Production
Female Hustler Part 4/by Joy Deja King
For complete Library of Congress Copyright info visit;

www.joydejaking.com
Twitter: @joydejaking

A King Production
P.O. Box 912, Collierville, TN 38027

A King Production and the above portrayal logo are trademarks of A King Production LLC.

This Book is Dedicated To My:

Family, Readers, and Supporters.
I LOVE you guys so much. Please believe that!!

—Joy Deja King

"I'm Not A Princess
I Don't Need Saving
I'm A Queen
I Got This Shit Handled…"

Angel

A KING PRODUCTION

All I See Is The Money...

Female 4
Hustler

A Novel

JOY DEJA KING

Chapter One

Cryin' In The Club

Angel's eyes were glued to the intense exchange between Dale and some stripper. She wondered why the woman was doing so much talking instead of dancing. Then a few seconds later, Dale bolted and he seemed to be enraged.

"Babe, I'll be right back. I see someone I need to discuss important business with," Angel said, giving Darien a quick kiss on the lips before walking off.

"Hurry back! I'm missing you already," he called out, thinking how badly he wanted to be inside his wife. He leaned back on the plush chair, drinking champagne; anxiously waiting for them to get back home, so he could rip off the sheer black Givenchy gown Angel was wearing.

Angel was rushing to stop the stripper Dale had been talking to before she lost her in the massive crowd. "Wait!" she shouted, but doubted the woman could hear her due to the throbbing music coming from the state-of-the-art sound system.

"What tha fuck!" the stripper snapped once Angel caught up with her and snatched her arm. "Why in the hell are you grabbing on me?!"

"I needed to get your attention," Angel stated.

"Well, you have it now... so what do you want?" The woman rolled her eyes and neck so hard, for a minute it looked like they were going to become stuck in that position.

"I'm Angel." The stripper was still ogling her like who tha fuck is you. "I'm partners with Desmond," Angel added since that was her boss.

The information did soften the woman's demeanor slightly, but not much. "Okay, but you still ain't told me why you grabbed on my arm like that?" she spat flinging her hand towards Angel as if dismissing her.

"My apologies... what's your name?"

"Nesa," she answered with a stank attitude.

"Nesa, I saw you speaking to Dale. There appeared to be a very heated conversation going on between you two. I wanted to make sure everything was okay."

"Everything is cool. We ain't got no problems, but umm, why you so concerned? Ain't that man 'bout to get married?"

"Yes, he is, to my sister."

Nesa's face frowned up, but she kept her cool. "Well, I suggest you go speak to the groom then, 'cause I ain't got shit else to say. Now if you would excuse me." Nesa perched her lips and shimmied off hard, as if to put an extra jiggle to her vast ass.

"I think I'll do that," Angel said out loud, deciding to go track Dale down since Nesa wasn't spilling shit. She rushed in the direction he was last seen going which was towards the back of the club.

"This can't be right," Angel mumbled under her breath. "I must've went through the wrong entryway," she continued, musing where the dark hallway would lead her. Her head was telling her to turn around, but her inner conscious seemed to be pulling her further down the obscure hallway.

Angel took a few more steps and noticed a flickering light on the floor. "That's odd," she commented walking closer to see where it was coming from. "What the hell!" she gasped noticing a woman slumped over in the corner across from where the flickering light was.

She bent down and lifted the woman up and blood got all over her hands. That's when Angel saw the gash on the back of her head. "I need to get you to the hospital!" Angel panicked and was talking out loud, trying to figure out who this woman was and how she ended up in the back of the club a bloody mess. She reached in her purse to dial 911, but got distracted. "What is that ticking sound?" Angel questioned, looking around to pinpoint where the sound was coming from. She gently put the woman back down and walked towards the ticking sound. It was coming from the same direction as the flickering light.

"Dear God, no! It's a bomb!" Angel screamed out. The bomb was placed directly in front of the door as if to guarantee no one could get out. She was tempted to pick it up and throw it outside, but wasn't sure if doing so would trigger it to detonate. "Oh gosh, what should I do?!" She was doing her best not to freak out, but Angel wasn't sure how much time she had, so it was imperative she act fast.

Angel ran over to the unconscious woman and began dragging her down the hallway, feeling relieved the young lady was so petite. She was pulling her as fast as she could while at the same time calling Darien.

"Come on, pick up!" she begged. "Fuck!" she yelled when Darien didn't answer. Undeterred, Angel called right back.

"Babe, where you at? I know you ain't leave without me," Darien cracked when he answered.

"Darien, there is a bomb in the club. Get everybody out of here now! Have the DJ make an announcement that everyone needs to evacuate."

"A bomb! Angel, you talkin' crazy!"

"No, I'm not! Darien, I'm dead ass serious! Get everybody the fuck outta here now!"

"Oh, shit! Where are you?"

"I'm on my way to the front of the club. I'll meet you outside," Angel told him.

"I'm not leaving without you! Tell me where you're at and I'll come to you. We can leave together," Darien insisted.

"We don't have time for that!" Angel yelled, scared and frustrated at the same time. "I'll meet you outside. Now clear this fuckin' club before we all die!"

Right after Angel ended the call with her husband, she immediately kicked off her heels. She needed to pick up her pace and Angel knew that would be impossible in some five-inch heels. As Angel got closer to the end of the hallway and was about to turn to walk through an entryway, she could hear the chaos erupting inside the club. Tables and chairs were knocked over. Broken glasses and champagne bottles were scattered throughout the floor. You could hear a mixture of yelling, heavy breathing, and cries echoing as if blasting from speakers in surround sound.

Angel struggled to push through the crowd, as patrons were practically knocking each other over in their quest to reach the exit door. Freedom seemed to be within arm's reach for Angel, but right before she could get out, there was a loud BOOM! The explosion ripped through the club destroying everything in sight.

Chapter Two

Set It Off

Taren smiled widely after detonating the bomb. She flung off her baseball cap and the long dark wig she had been wearing. "Damn, that shit was hot," she complained, rubbing her fingers through her cropped blonde hair. Taren turned up the radio and began bopping her head. She was rapping along to the lyrics of the trap music like she didn't have a care in the world. As cars drove by, no one would ever think the young lady driving a non-descript rental car, just set off a bomb at Diamonds & Pearls strip club.

In the midst of her driving and rapping, Taren came up with an idea to further cover her tracks, in case someone questioned her. She decided to send Angel a text.

Hey Girl! I was on my way to the club when Aunt Flo made an unexpected visit ☹ ***Between that and my stomach cramping, I'm in for the night. Enjoy the party! Talk to you 2morrow. Love you!***

Taren felt confident she had it all figured out. She continued her ride home thinking to herself that revenge sure tasted sweet.

Angel's ears were ringing after the blast went off. It felt like a wave was pushing her as a gust hit her in the back, pinning her against the wall. It took her a few minutes to realize where she was or remember what happened.

"Fuck," Angel muttered. Her head was throbbing and the room felt like it was spinning. When she was finally able to focus, Angel was horrified to see bloody, lifeless bodies scattered on the club's floor. She was having difficulty standing up so Angel grabbed onto the edge of a table that was next to her.

"Where am I?" Angel heard someone babble. It was dark and smoky so it was hard for her to decipher where the voice was coming from. The moaning was getting louder as Angel began walking to try and find a way out of the club.

"I can't see shit in here," Angel scoffed, being careful where she walked. When she stepped on something that felt hard but small she bent down to see what it was. "A phone. I can use this to give me a little bit of light," she said pressing down on the home button of the iPhone. Angel continued to walk in the direction of the moaning using the phone as a flashlight. "It's you!" she shouted. She bent down when she realized the moaning was coming from the woman she'd found passed out near the bomb.

"Help me. Somebody help me," she uttered.

"I'm right here," Angel said shining the light from the phone in the woman's face. "What's your name?"

"Dominique."

"Dominique, I'm Angel. There was an explosion. If help isn't already outside, I'm sure they're on the way. I'ma go see if I can find a way out. I'll be back."

"Don't leave me... please." Dominique put her hand on Angel's wrist. "I don't want to be left alone. Don't go," she pleaded.

"Okay. I'll stay here with you." Angel couldn't sit there doing nothing so she had to try and find out what was going on. Although she didn't know the password to use the iPhone, she could place an emergency call.

"Hi, my name is Angel and I'm trapped in the Diamonds & Pearls nightclub on Biscayne Blvd. There was a bomb explosion."

"Yes, we're aware of the situation and firefighters and emergency crews are in route," the 911 operator informed Angel.

"Do you know how long it will be before they get us out? I'm with a woman that needs immediate medical attention. There are also several bodies on the floor and I don't know if they are dead or alive."

"We understand the severity and a rescue team will be there shortly. I can stay on the phone with you until they arrive if it will help keep you calm."

"I can stay calm on my own," Angel snapped. "Hopefully they'll get us outta here sooner than later. Thanks!" Angel huffed and ended the call.

"What did they say... is help on the way?" Dominique questioned. Her voice was becoming faint as if she was about to pass out again.

"Yes. Try to relax. Help will be here soon and we'll get you to a hospital. I promise." Angel prayed that was one promise she would be able to keep as she held Dominique's limp hand.

"What tha fuck happened?!" Aaliyah yelled out to Justina who was also in the bathroom with her.

"That noise was like a sharp bang and then a long, thundering growl. That's the sound of a bomb," Justina said trying to open the bathroom door.

"Gosh, why didn't we stay our asses outside instead of coming back in here to use the restroom," Aaliyah huffed.

"Something must be blocking the door because it's not budging." Justina leaned her back against the wall, slowly sliding down in defeat.

"This is some straight up bullshit! It's my fuckin' engagement party and I'm stuck in a dark ass bathroom. Well at least I'm stuck in here with my best friend, right..."

"Good point, but we need to get the hell outta here!" Justina belted as she banged on the door.

"And my phone is getting no service," Aaliyah complained.

"Mine either. Between the explosion and the bathroom being downstairs, I figured service would be nonexistent."

"You have a point. If you're right and that was a bomb we heard, then it probably exploded upstairs on the main floor." Aaliyah covered her mouth as the severity of the situation kicked in. "Oh gosh, I hope Dale is okay and everyone else. Do you think people are dead upstairs?" Aaliyah cringed at the thought.

"If that was a bomb, more than likely yes."

"Who would want to blow up this club? I mean, I know this can't be an act of terrorism... what can it be? Does this Desmond dude have a lot of enemies?"

Aaliyah, shut the fuck up! When the bomb exploded, too bad it didn't knock ya ass out, Justina thought to herself. "I have no clue. I guess we won't get any answers until we get outta here."

"When will that be? I'm kinda claustrophobic. Soon I'll start hyperventilating if that door doesn't open," Aaliyah said, sighing.

Of course, Princess Aaliyah will be stricken with a panic attack and start hyperventilating if she isn't saved. Boohoo. That's the least of her worries. If they don't get us out of here soon and I'm stuck with her whiny ass, I'ma kill her myself, Justina said to herself as she rolled her eyes then began pounding on the door. She was hoping someone would hear them because being trapped in a bathroom with Aaliyah felt like a death sentence to Justina.

Chapter Three

Blowing Smoke

Amir was up late, looking over some stock stats on his iPhone, when a text came through from one of his associates telling him to check TMZ. Amir wasn't into pop culture as time didn't allow it. He was much too consumed with handling the family's drug operation. But his associate knew that, so he figured it must be of some importance.

The leading story said breaking news and Amir immediately recognized the club Diamond &

Pearls in Miami being the venue where Aaliyah was having her engagement party. There was a picture and video showing the club collapsed and in flames. Right away he tried calling Justina and Aaliyah. His call went straight to voicemail. His next thought was to call his father, but his parents were out of the country on a romantic getaway so they could reconnect after being kept apart for so many years. His next option was to call either Nico or Precious; he opted on Nico.

"You ain't in jail are you?" Nico asked sounding half asleep.

"Nah."

"Then why the hell you calling me so late?"

"It's about Aaliyah, I think she might be in trouble," Amir told him.

"Trouble... what kind of trouble." Nico began coming out of his stupor.

"There was some sort of explosion at the club tonight where she had her engagement party. I haven't been able to get her or Justina on the phone."

"Dear God! Angel was at that party too!" Nico was now all the way up, getting out of his bed. I'ma make some phone calls and see what I can find out. You call Precious. Tell her what's going on and that we'll need to use Supreme's private jet. We don't have time to wait for a commercial flight. We heading to Miami tonight," Nico said without hesitation.

"I'm on it!" Amir knew if he couldn't get his dad on the line, Nico was the next best option. He would know exactly what the next move should be without missing a beat.

"Stay with me!" Angel repeatedly said, gently tapping the side of Dominique's face but she'd passed back out. To make matters worse, the phone she had been using was about to die at any moment and having that little bit of light made her situation somewhat bearable.

"Dominique, hold tight. I'll be right back. I'ma try and find another phone before this one dies," she said out loud just in case there was even a slight chance she could hear her. Angel hated to leave Dominique as she felt connected to her in a strange way, but felt it was necessary to locate another phone.

Between the dead bodies, shattered glass, and a semi-collapsed building, it was difficult for Angel to identify anything, let alone a small ass smart phone. She kept moving ahead though, praying she would get some sort of sign. Before long, Angel was on the other side of the room and still hadn't found anything, but she did hear a slight banging noise.

She put the phone up to get a clear view what was ahead of her and saw some stairs that led to the lower level. When she got closer to the stairs the banging sound became louder.

When Angel reached the bottom of the stairs she knew the banging was coming from inside the women's bathroom. "Hey! Are you okay in there?" Angel called out.

"Yes! Can you please get us out!" Justina yelled.

"Hurry! Hurry! I'm having a hard time breathing!" Aaliyah wheezed, feeling very light-headed.

"Aaliyah, is that you?!" Angel questioned, thinking that the voice sounded familiar.

"Yes! It's me, Aaliyah! Who are you?"

"It's me, Angel!"

"Angel! Please get me outta here! There's a lot of smoke and I'm really dizzy. I think I might faint. Please open the door."

"This is Justina! I'm in here too!" she yelled out, sensing Aaliyah was only concerned about herself.

"Try to relax and give me a minute. I'm by myself and there are some tables and chairs blocking the door. There's no one else to help me, but I will get the both of you out."

Angel knew it would take a lot of work, but she refused to be defeated. She was concerned about how out of breath Aaliyah sounded. That was her sister and she would do whatever necessary to get that door open.

Taren was a habitual blunt smoker, but when she was panicky or feeling on edge, she would pull out a Newport and chain-smoke all day and night. She was now on her sixth cigarette and reaching for number seven as she flipped through the channels seeing if there was any news about the club explosion.

"Where the hell is the breaking news!" she barked, tossing the remote control down on the couch. Taren was now pacing the floor, as she was desperate to find out if her plan was effective. "Damn, I hope Angel was blown up in a million little pieces," Taren muttered taking another pull from the Newport.

Knock... knock... knock

"Who the hell is that!? Oh, goodness that ain't the police coming to arrest me is it?" Taren was biting down on her lip as her paranoia was kicking in. "Maybe if I ignore them, they'll go away."

Knock... knock... knock...

But the knocking persisted and got louder. Now Taren was biting down on her nails and getting jittery like she was on some crack head shit.

"Taren, are you there! Taren!"

"That ain't the police," Taren mouthed, feeling relieved as she went to open the door.

"Omigosh, Taren! Have you heard?!" Monique barged in frantically. "What took you so long to answer the door?" she questioned. "This is an emergency!"

Shut yo' annoying ass up. Why ain't you at that damn club? I wanted you to blow up in that explosion too, Taren thought to herself, but played nice instead. Since Monique was still alive, if shit hit the fan, Taren wanted to have at least one ally.

"I was using the bathroom. When I came out I heard the banging and immediately opened the door. Why don't you sit down," Taren suggested, taking Monique's hand. "You seem so upset. What happened... can I get you something to drink?"

"Yes, please. Do you have any wine? No... no! Just give me some water. I need to keep a clear head," Monique said nervously, tugging on her limp straight hair.

"Of course. So, what happened?" Taren asked, already knowing the answer, walking to the kitchen. "And why aren't you at that party they were having at the club tonight?"

"Thank goodness I didn't go! What about you? Why didn't you go?"

"Cramps. I was getting dressed and then it

came on. I was disappointed I couldn't make, but it sounds like it was a blessing in disguise," Taren said, handing Monique a bottle of water.

"It was! A bomb went off at the club!"

"A bomb! You can't be serious?"

"Dead serious! Amber called me. She was able to get out right before the bomb went off. She was the one that told me she didn't see you there. I tried calling you, but you didn't answer."

"Yeah, my phone is charging. I didn't know you were trying to reach me."

"I decided to just come over and tell you what happened, especially since Angel didn't make it out," Monique blurted out before bursting into tears. "I know how close the two of you are," she said, shaking her head.

Taren covered her mouth and gave her best shocked, despondent, and stunned impression. "It's a mistake. I spoke with Angel through text message. She was at the party and everything was going fine. There's no way she got caught up in an explosion. Amber has to be wrong!"

"I'm so sorry, Taren, but it's true," Monique sniffed. "If it isn't already, I'm sure it will be on the news because it's all over the blogs."

"And you're sure Angel didn't make it out safely?" Taren wanted to confirm before she began celebrating in her head.

"Positive," Monique stated somberly.

"How did Amber get out and not Angel?"

"I wasn't able to talk to Amber long because the place was swarmed with cops. They wanted to interview everyone and see who needed medical attention. But from what she told me, they got a warning to get out right before the bomb went off. A lot of people were able to leave, but some didn't exit in time. Unfortunately, Angel was one of those people." The faucet of tears began once again. Taren figured they were coming, so she already had gotten some tissue and handed it to Monique.

"Maybe we should drive over there," Taren hinted, wanting to get an up-close view of her work.

"I don't think that's a good idea. I'm sure they have the street blocked off by now anyway."

"We can park the car and walk the rest of the way." Taren was not backing off her sick need to see the damage she had caused. She went so far as to get her flip flops from the closet in the hallway and put on a baseball cap. Taren was dressed and ready to exit out the front door.

From the scowl on Monique's face, it was obvious she wasn't about to cosign on Taren's idea. "We should wait here. I can only imagine how chaotic it is, we don't need to add to it."

"You're probably right." Taren felt she needed to back down. If she opted to keep pushing the matter, she worried Monique might become wary. "I feel helpless sitting in this apartment doing nothing. In my heart I know Angel needs me."

'This has to be so hard on you," Monique said, rubbing Taren's back. "It's devastating to me too. What sort of sinister person can blow up a club with innocent people inside," she continued, shaking her head. "They better catch this monster, lock 'em up, and throw away the key."

Taren sat silently while Monique went on her rant. Instead of talking, she listened and laughed to herself at how pathetic she thought Monique sounded. *They'll never catch me. I've outsmarted all you idiots. While Angel is burning in hell, I'll be out in these streets living my life and enjoying my freedom.* It took all of Taren's strength not to allow a wide smile to spread across her face.

Chapter Four

High Stakes

As the pilot prepared to take off from the Teterboro Airport in New Jersey, Nico, Amir, and Precious sat on the private jet, all in deep thought. Precious was shaken out of hers when she glanced down at her phone and noticed Supreme was calling.

"Hey, babe," she answered.

"Any news on Aaliyah?" was Supreme's first question.

"No. But we're on the plane now, about to take

off at any moment."

"Call me when you land. I'm taking a flight out of LA first thing in the morning. If you find out anything before I get to Miami, let me know."

"I will. She has to be okay, Supreme... she just has to be," Precious said, closing her eyes.

"I know. We have to pray that she is. I'll talk to you soon."

"Did you thank Supreme for me? For letting us use his jet?" Nico asked when he saw Precious was off the phone.

"No, there was no need. You know Supreme loves Aaliyah just as much as we do." Precious cut her eyes at Nico. "After all these years, you still try to take pot shots at Supreme, whenever you can."

Amir frowned up his face, knowing the tongue lashing between these two was about to get intense and he wasn't in the mood.

"I didn't mean to offend you, Precious. I do know that Supreme cares deeply for our daughter."

"You just had to stress 'our' daughter. She's Supreme's daughter too," Precious shot back. "Having the same DNA isn't the only criteria for being a mother or a father. Just ask all the parents of adopted children."

"I'm not minimizing Supreme's role in Aaliyah's life, but I am her biological father. I'm sure you're not disputing that."

"No disrespect," Amir jumped in and said before the banter between them could continue, "but can we please not do this. We all love Aaliyah. Let's put our energy into the idea that she's okay and that Justina's okay, too."

"And my daughter Angel," Nico was quick to add.

"Yes, my apologies and your daughter Angel," Amir said, hoping to put an end to any bickering.

"Nico, I totally forgot that Angel went to Aaliyah's engagement party. I'm so sorry," Precious said sincerely. "I pray she's okay, too."

"Thank you. My daughters are all I have. I don't know what I would do if I lost either one of them," Nico admitted gravely.

"Let's pray you'll never find out." Amir yearned staring out the window, as the jet took off into the darkness.

"I'm starting to feel like I'm suffocating." Aaliyah coughed, becoming sick from inhaling all the smoke.

"I know what you mean," Justina agreed. She banged on the door again, but with a lot less arm power. Her energy level was starting to deplete also. "Please hurry, Angel," she managed to say.

"I'm almost done!" Angel yelled out. The objects blocking the door were much heavier than Angel anticipated. She also didn't understand what was taking so long for the rescue team to get inside the club. Yes, it was massive and there was a lot of damage, but it felt to Angel like it was taking them forever. Part of the reason she felt like that was because of the hard work she was putting in to get Aaliyah and Justina out. Then she was concerned about Dominique, feeling guilty she had left her alone. But Angel wouldn't allow her mind to ponder on that right now. Getting her sister out was her number one priority.

"Finally!" Angel let out a deep sigh. When she opened the bathroom door both Aaliyah and Justina were slumped against the wall. She remembered seeing some bottles of water near the bar while moving it. She quickly went over and grabbed some, then came back into the bathroom.

"The door is open," Justina was the first to notice.

"Yes, here take this." Angel handed Justina the water before going over to check on Aaliyah. "Here, drink this water." Angel put it up to Aaliyah's mouth and after a few gulps a burst of strength took over and she was able to hold the bottle herself.

"Thank you," Aaliyah said after drinking all the water.

"Do you hear that?!" Justina had optimism in her voice. Angel and Aaliyah both went silent to check if they heard anything too. At first, they didn't, but then there was a loud noise.

"Do you think another bomb went off?!" Aaliyah panicked.

"No, I bet it's the rescue team. They probably found a way to finally get in," Angel figured.

"Well, let's go! We need to get upstairs so they don't leave us!" Justina yelled, standing up.

"Come on, Aaliyah." She was still a little weak so Angel helped her stand up. Justina was already out the door as Angel waited for Aaliyah to get her balance.

"I'm okay." She nodded, feeling she could walk on her own.

"Are you sure?"

"Yeah."

It wasn't that dark in the bathroom, but once they entered the lobby area, Aaliyah used the light from the phone so they could get to the stairs without any problems.

"Where's Justina?" Aaliyah wanted to know.

"She might already be upstairs," Angel said until she saw what appeared to be a female figure standing over something in the corner. "Justina, is that you!" Angel called out.

"Yes!" she quickly turned around and headed

towards them.

"What were you doing over there?" Angel questioned.

"Oh, it's nothing. I saw a body over there." Justina nodded her head in the direction she just came from. "I wanted to see if they were alive so I could help, but unfortunately she's dead."

"Are you sure? Maybe she's just unconscious," Angel said walking off to go check.

"I'm positive!" Justina reached over and grabbed Angel's arm. "I checked her pulse, she didn't have one."

"Come on you guys, we need to get outta here! I think the ceiling is starting to crack," Aaliyah said, holding her phone up, shining the light.

"Yeah, she's right!" Justina agreed. "We better hurry!"

The three women hurried towards the stairs. As they got closer, the ceiling began cracking even more, but something was holding Angel back.

"You guys go ahead. I'll meet you upstairs." Angel told them.

"Where are you going?" Aaliyah was puzzled.

"I forgot my phone in the bathroom. I need to go back and get it. It will only take me a second. I'll be fine. Go ahead and go upstairs so the rescue team will know we're here."

"Come on! She'll be fine." Justina latched onto

Aaliyah's wrist pulling her forward. Aaliyah reluctantly went with Justina. She didn't want to leave Angel, but she had faith her sister would make it upstairs in time.

Chapter Five

Welcome To The Breakdown

Precious, Amir, and Nico went directly from the airport to Diamond & Pearls nightclub. Lucky for them, their driver was a retired cop, which enabled them to get pass the police barricade. Once they arrived, it was even more chaotic then any of them had imagined. It was almost impossible to maneuver with all the fire trucks, police cars, and ambulances.

"Has anyone seen my daughter Aaliyah?" While Precious was asking anyone she passed that question, Nico and Amir were speaking to police officers, trying to get answers.

At this point, Precious retrieved a recent photo of Aaliyah from her phone and was showing it to everybody.

"Excuse me!"

Precious felt someone tap her on the shoulder. "Yes!"

"I don't know your daughter, but I do know her sister."

"You're talking about Angel? Is Aaliyah with her?" Precious wanted to know.

"I hope she isn't with her."

"Why... why would you say that?" Precious's heart began beating rapidly. The young lady she was speaking to seemed more like the bearer of bad news then good.

"Police aren't any help. Did you find out anything?" Nico ran up to Precious asking.

"This young lady knows Angel," Precious informed him.

"You know my daughter Angel... is she okay?"

"Who are you?"

"I'm her father."

"Angel spoke so highly of you. Finding her father changed her life. She was the happiest I'd ever seen her. I'm sorry, I'm rambling on. I should probably introduce myself. I'm Amber. I had the pleasure of working for your daughter."

"Thank you for the insight, Amber. Now can you tell me where my daughter is?"

"In there." Amber pointed to the demolished building and began crying. "She didn't make it out in time."

"Are you sure?!" Nico's eyes instantly watered up.

"Yes. Her husband was trying to go back in the club once he realized she was still inside. He was going crazy out here."

"Where is Darien now?" Nico asked.

"The police ended up arresting him because he wouldn't back down. Darien said he would rather die than leave Angel in there," Amber wailed.

"What about Aaliyah?" Precious lifted Amber's chin up. She knew the girl was hurting and felt bad for her and Nico, but she wanted to find her daughter.

"The last time I saw Aaliyah," Amber managed to say between weeps, "was inside the club, before the explosion."

"You never saw her out here with everyone else?" Precious pressed.

Amber shook her head no as the tears continued to flow.

Precious turned to Nico who was on the verge of cracking. "I can't speak on Angel, but Aaliyah isn't dead. I would be able to feel it right here," Precious placed her hand over her heart before continuing, "if my baby girl didn't survive."

As if God knew Precious was about to have a nervous breakdown and pass out right there in the middle of the street, He answered her prayers.

"Look!" Nico shouted, pointing at what used to be the front entrance of the club. "Aaliyah and Justina just came out." They rushed towards them, moving folks out the way so they could get by.

"My baby is okay!" Precious cried, holding Aaliyah tightly in her arms. Then it was Nico's turn to embrace his daughter.

"Thank God you're okay."

"I'm fine, Dad. With all the craziness I've been through, this is definitely in the top three."

"I can only imagine how afraid you must've been; a bomb exploding in a club. What is this world coming to?" Precious shook her head in dismay.

"Aaliyah, did you see Angel while you were in there?" Nico questioned, not willing to give up hope in finding his other daughter.

"Yes, Daddy I did."

"Where is she... please tell me she's okay."

"She went back to get her phone. I told her to come with us, but she insisted we go on without her and that she would meet us upstairs," Aaliyah's voice cracked.

"It's true, Mr. Carter."

"Nobody asked you, Justina!" Nico barked. He then peered into Aaliyah's eyes. "You left Angel in there alone. She's your sister!" he yelled.

"Nico, calm down." Precious placed her hand on his shoulder. He shrugged her off him and walked over to the sidewalk, sitting on the curb.

"That look Daddy gave me. He's never looked at me like that before. He hates me," Aaliyah cried.

"Your father could never hate you." Precious held her daughter, wanting to comfort her. "Nico is worried about Angel which is understandable, but it's not your fault that she went back for her phone."

"But she got me and Justina out of the bathroom. The door was stuck, Mom. We wouldn't have gotten out without her." Aaliyah covered her face in despair. "The ceiling was about to fall down on us as we were heading upstairs. I should've insisted she come with us instead of going to get some dumb phone!" Guilt was weighing heavy on Aaliyah as she continued to cry in her mother's arms.

"The building is about to completely collapse!" one of the firefighters announced to the emergency crews. "We have to clear out. I believe all the survivors have been rescued. We'll go back in and get the remaining dead bodies once it's safe."

When they heard the news, Precious and Aaliyah turned to Nico and he was done. "I don't think I've ever seen Daddy cry. I have to go be with him!"

Precious grabbed Aaliyah's arm and yanked her back before she could get away. "Give your father a moment."

"Let me go! He needs me!" Aaliyah insisted.

"NO!" Precious said firmly. "What he needs is time alone. You will stay right here. He has to process this, Aaliyah. Yes, your father needs you, but not right now." Precious refused to budge. She was a parent and unlike Aaliyah, Precious knew exactly the sort of pain Nico was in at this very moment.

"Fine." Aaliyah wiped away her tears, hating to give in to her mother's demands, but she didn't have a choice.

"Talk about a night of miracles," Precious said in disbelief. Her eyes widened when she recognized Angel coming out the rubble carrying, somewhat dragging, a woman that was much taller and bigger than her.

"Daddy! Daddy! Look it's Angel!" Aaliyah shouted with enthusiasm when she saw what caused her mother's mouth to drop in amazement.

"I cannot believe Angel carried Nesa out. I thought I left that bitch for dead," Justina mumbled, watching from a distance as they all ran towards Angel.

"Baby! You're okay!" Amir lifted Justina up in the air, completely catching her off guard.

"Amir, I had no idea you were here." She smiled, giving him a kiss.

"Yeah, one of the rescue workers I was speaking with on the other side of the building had a list of names of some of the people that had been taken to the hospital. I was checking to see if any of your names were on there. Of course, that wasn't the case and now I see why." He grinned, returning the kiss. "Man, am I thrilled to be holding you. Have you seen Precious and Nico... are Aaliyah and Angel okay?"

"Yes, to both of your questions. If you look to your left, the happy family is all together." Justina gave Amir her best fake smile.

"Thank God. We were all so worried. I'm always thinking something bad is gonna go down because of the line of business I'm in. Now, I have to be concerned with my loved ones going to a party at a club. Crazy world we're living in," Amir scoffed.

"You're right. We are living in a crazy world and I have the feeling it's only going to get crazier," Justina stated as her plotting began.

Chapter Six

Liability

"We have to stop meeting like this," Angel joked, sitting up in her hospital bed, grinning at her father.

"This isn't funny, young lady. You and Aaliyah are going to send me to an early grave. I can't take any more stress... don't you see all this gray in my hair?" Nico laughed.

"The gray is hard to miss, but it also makes you look very distinguished," Angel said, winking. "So distinguished and handsome that I bet, if you went and talked to my nurse, you could convince her to discharge me from the hospital right now."

"I dislike hospitals too, but you only have a few more days. You suffered a lot of smoke inhalation. The doctor wants to monitor you a little bit longer to make sure you don't suffer a setback."

"Listen to you getting all medical." Angel smirked. "I know it's for the best, but I'm ready to get home and back to my life."

"That will happen soon enough, but don't rush things. You've been through a lot, Angel. Even heroes have to take a day off."

"I'm not a hero."

"Not only did you save your sister and Justina, but you also saved that woman you carried out the building. That sounds like a hero to me," Nico said proudly.

"Doing the right thing doesn't make someone a hero. I wish I could've done more. I can't get my mind off that woman, Dominique, who I found unconscious before the bomb went off. Did you find out anything, Dad?"

"I'm sorry, no one has any information on a woman named Dominque. But several of the people they brought in had no ID, so she could be here. You have to give it time, Angel. You need to concentrate on getting better which means getting some rest."

"Your father's right," Darien said walking into

the room with a beautiful bouquet of flowers.

"Never would I think you'd agree with anything I had to say," Nico mocked. "I see you brought my lovely daughter even more flowers. Can you at least leave enough space in here for her old man to bring her some more."

"Sorry, Nico, but I can't help myself."

"Nothing wrong with that. You're a man in love. Just make sure you keep treating my daughter right." Nico kissed Angel on the forehead. "Now, you young lady better listen to your father. Get some rest. I'll be back tomorrow."

"Yes, Daddy, I will follow your orders."

"Good. I love you."

"I love you, too. See you tomorrow."

"Darien." Nico nodded, walking past him on his way out.

"Nico." Darien nodded back.

"It's nice to see you and my father being cordial to one another." Angel beamed kissing her husband on the lips before taking her flowers. "I don't think I'll ever get tired of the scent of fresh flowers," she said taking another whiff.

"Hope not because I have another delivery coming later today."

"I love how you spoil me."

"You make it easy. I really don't deserve you as a wife. Luckily, that didn't stop you from marrying me."

"We're both lucky. Speaking of lucky, how is Dale doing? I didn't have a chance to ask my father and Aaliyah hasn't been here for a couple of days."

"It's probably because they transferred Dale to another hospital where they specialize in head trauma," Darien revealed.

"Is he still unconscious?"

"Yep."

"Poor Aaliyah. Less than a week ago she was celebrating at her engagement party and now she's keeping a vigil by her fiancé's bedside. Life can be so unfair." Angel sighed.

"I do feel bad for her. For the brief time I spent with Dale, he seemed like a real cool dude. I'm praying he pulls through."

"Me too."

"I'm grateful you're alright though," Darien said, sitting on the edge of the bed right next to Angel. "I don't think I would want to live if you weren't here to grow old with me."

"Baby, don't talk like that. I am here and whether you like it or not, we're growing old together. You'll be stuck with me, wrinkles and all," Angel teased.

"Sounds like music to my ears."

Taren observed from the door as the couple gushed over one another. The entire scene made her stomach turn. She made sure not to utter a sound not wanting to make her presence known just yet.

Instead, Taren began orchestrating her next move. It burnt her to the core that Angel not only survived the explosion, but her loved ones were showering her with attention and adoration. It seemed Angel could do no wrong and that infuriated Taren. The more things went right in her former best friend's life, the more Taren became unhinged.

"Yo, this muthafuckin' shit needs to be handled!" Desmond roared, ready to punch his fist through the glass window in his downtown Miami office.

"Desmond, you gotta relax. I got you covered," Miles stood up from the leather sofa and said.

"What about Dominique? Have you found out anything?"

"No." Miles hated to admit, putting his head down.

"This shit is crazy. Dominique fuckin' vanishes, the club gets blown up," Desmond huffed, breathing heavily.

"Chill, I got this. The best men within the organization are working on this. We gon' find out who tha fuck is responsible for that bomb going off. You have to trust me," Miles asserted.

"It's not about trust. I was running a lucrative

operation and what I spent years building blew up in smoke within a matter of seconds." Desmond's jaw was flinching. His anger had been on ten since the night of the explosion and it hasn't subsided since.

"Whoever did this will pay with their life. It don't matter how many muthafuckers were involved... we gettin' them all," Miles spit.

"Yeah, you handle that while I focus on gettin' Diamonds & Pearls back open."

"So soon?" Miles was surprised.

"You can't leave no money on the table. If I don't reopen soon, my girls are gonna have to find work elsewhere. They have to eat too. Every stripper I know has already spent the money they made for the night. A savings account ain't even in they vocabulary."

"Do you have a spot in mind?"

"I'm looking at a couple of potential locations tomorrow. I'll keep looking until I find the right spot."

"Cool, while you handling yo' business I'll be handling mine."

"Good 'cause these cops seem fuckin' clueless. They don't have any suspects and supposedly the one camera that is aimed in the direction of the alley wasn't working. So they don't know who came through that back door and left the bomb there."

"That shit is fucked up." Miles shook his head.

"The good thing is, all muthafuckers talk. I don't care who they is, at some point, they'll get diarrhea of the mouth and spill it all. I might have to be patient, but a snake always come slithering out from the dark. We just have to be ready." Desmond stood in front of the window with his hands in his pockets, staring out at the Miami skyline. He didn't like the rage that was bubbling inside of him. Desmond considered himself to be a strategic man, but he knew anger could easily blur that line, causing him to make reckless decisions. It was going to take all of Desmond's self-control to avoid that from happening.

"Can I come in?" Taren smiled. She waited until Darien had left and was on the elevator before coming into Angel's room. Taren wanted her alone without any distractions.

"Omigosh, Taren! It's so good to see you. Come give me a hug!"

"You look great," Taren said after their embrace.

"Oh, please. I expect my husband to tell me that lie, but not my best friend." Angel laughed. "Sit down. I've missed having girl talk with a close friend."

"It seems you've had plenty of visitors," Taren commented, looking around the room.

"Most of these flowers are from Darien. Yes, a few other people sent me some, including you." Angel playfully tapped Taren's leg. "Thank you so much. I wanted to call you, but my dad and Darien took away all devices. They wanted me to rest, so I'm thrilled you came to visit."

"I wanted to see you as soon as I found out. I've been so worried. I feel guilty that I didn't come to the party. Maybe I could've gotten you out before the explosion."

"Why didn't you come?" Angel questioned.

"You didn't get my text?"

"No."

"While I was getting dressed, I got an unexpected visitor in the form of the color red." Taren giggled.

"Say no more. Trust me it worked out in your favor and please don't you dare feel guilty. The only person responsible for this tragedy is the sadist who left that bomb."

"Do the cops have any idea who did it? I mean what kind of person would blow up a club? Do they think it was a terrorist?"

"I have no idea. Two detectives came to talk to me a few days ago, but they were mainly asking questions instead of answering any. They did make one comment I thought was interesting."

"What was that?"

"The bomb was powerful, but it wasn't sophisticatedly made, as if done by an amateur."

"That is interesting."

"But if they could find this woman, I believe she could give them a good lead," Angel said.

"What woman?" Taren was trying to sound concerned instead of afraid of being caught.

"I found this woman unconscious by the bomb. I can't shake this feeling that the two are somehow linked."

"So where is this woman?"

"I have no clue and it's so frustrating. She told me her name was Dominique."

"Do you have any water in here?" Taren asked, feeling like the walls were closing in on her.

"Yeah, there's a pitcher and some cups right over there on the table." Angel pointed in the direction of the table as she continued talking. "After the bomb went off, she regained consciousness for a little while. That's when she told me her name. Then she passed back out and I had to leave her which I felt horrible about."

"I'm sure you would've stayed with her if you could've," Taren said, pouring herself another cup of water.

"Of course, but honestly if I had stayed with

her then I probably wouldn't have been able to save Aaliyah and Justina. That doesn't make my guilt go away. I just can't understand why no one can find her unless…"

"Unless what?"

"She's one of the unidentified dead bodies." Angel hated to even let her mind go there, but she knew it was a real possibility.

"That would be terrible if the woman you helped turned out to be dead." Taren sounded sympathetic to Angel's feelings of guilt.

"That's why I'm praying she's still alive. Not only because she seemed like a sweet girl, but what if she does know who left that bomb."

"Angel, you don't even know her. You said yourself she was unconscious for most of the time you were with her. How do you know if she's a sweet girl?"

"It was a feeling or maybe it was the way she said don't leave me. Or, the way she held my hand."

"Angel, you really need to get your rest," Taren said wanting to put an end to her emotional sermon over Dominique. "All this worrying can't be good for you."

"I'm fine. When I get out this hospital one of the first things I'm going to do is find out what happened to Dominique. Even if she is dead, I'm sure she has family that loves her. They would want to make sure she had a proper burial."

"Always gotta be the hero," Taren mumbled under her breath.

"I didn't hear you... what did you say?"

"I just said you're always so sweet," Taren lied while she fluffed Angel's pillow. "Now you get some rest. I'll be back tomorrow to visit and bring you a cupcake from that bakery you love."

"You're the best!" Angel beamed. "Thanks again for stopping by and listening to me ramble on."

"That's what best friends are for. See you soon." Taren kissed Angel on the cheek then waved goodbye.

Once Taren was outside Angel's hospital room, she wanted to flip over the steel and plastic medical trolley in front of her. *I knew I should've put a bullet in her head! Dominique is the only thing linking me to that bomb. Why didn't I kill her when I had the opportunity? Now there's a chance she could still be alive. Instead of focusing on getting rid of Angel, I have to put my energy on finding out what happened to Dominique before the police or anyone else tracks her down,* Taren thought to herself as she rushed out the hospital.

Chapter Seven

Say Don't Go

"Aaliyah, come back to the hotel with me. Or we can go to your place, but you must get out this hospital. Being here every day and every night isn't going to bring Dale out of his coma," Precious told her daughter.

"Don't you think I know that!" Aaliyah snapped. "But in case he does wake up, I want to be the first face he sees."

"I understand, but you have to keep your

strength up. When is the last time you even had a hot meal? Baby, I think you've lost ten pounds in the past week," Precious said, noticing that the skinny jeans her daughter was wearing appeared to be more of a loose fit on her normally slim but curvy frame.

Aaliyah rolled her eyes not wanting to engage in this conversation with her mother. "I know you mean well, but I don't need this," she sneered turning away as Supreme was walking up.

"Where is Aaliyah hurrying off to?"

"Far away from me." Precious's lips turned down in a grimace. "I suggested she leave the hospital, eat a real meal, and get some rest. The way she reacted, you would've thought I told her to abandon Dale. Maybe she'll listen to you," Precious said shrugging.

"She's scared, that's all. I'll go talk to her," Supreme said, kissing Precious before following after Aaliyah.

"Kids!" Precious sighed, pacing the hospital hallway. "Do I really feel like taking this call?" She debated and decided to answer. "Hello, Nico."

"Hello to you, too. How's Aaliyah?"

"The same. I don't think we'll see a change in her until we get a change in Dale's condition."

"What is the doctor saying?"

"Not much. He believes Dale is going to wake

up, but there are no guarantees in terms of his condition."

"I'm sure Aaliyah isn't taking that well."

"You know how she is. Automatically, her mind is thinking the worse. At this point, all I can do is be here for her because Dale waking up is the only thing she's interested in, plus Aaliyah's stubborn."

"So says the most stubborn woman I know."

"Nico, is there something else you wanted?" Precious hissed.

"Yes. The private investigator I hired to work this case came across some vital information."

"Really?! Tell me more." Precious walked over to a lounge that was nearby and sat down. Whoever was responsible for ruining her daughter's engagement party, she wanted them brought to their knees.

"There was a business across the street that had a camera aimed directly towards an alley by the club. I retrieved the video before the cops got ahold of it."

"How did you pull that off?"

"I had to pay a hefty price, but the business owner handed the footage over to my P.I. and told the police the camera wasn't working."

"Nice work, Mr. Carter." Precious smiled. "Have you viewed the video yet?"

"Yes. Before the explosion went off, two women are seen going into the club using a side door. A few minutes later, one of the women comes out, then less than ten minutes later the bomb goes off."

"Are you saying a woman is responsible for that explosion?" Precious asked in utter shock.

"Based on that footage, I would say yes."

"Could you see their faces?"

"No, only the back and a slight side view of one of the women. But they seemed familiar with the club so I'm taking the footage over to Desmond Blackwell's office so he can have a look."

"Who is Desmond Blackwell?"

"The owner of Diamonds & Pearls. I'm thinking maybe one or both women worked for the club. He might be able to identify them," Nico reasoned.

"Hopefully you're right. But why would a woman want to blow up a nightclub? Do you think she was working for somebody and this was a retaliation against this Desmond guy?"

"Could be. I had my P.I. do some research on Mr. Blackwell and he's definitely involved in some questionable business dealings. But if we get the girl, I think we'll find out everything we need to know," Nico stated confidently.

"You gave me exactly what I needed," Amir moaned,

sliding out of Justina. "I could lay in this bed next to you all day," he said while the ceiling fan blew cool air on his sweaty body.

"Does that mean I left you satisfied?"

"Completely. So much so that if I don't get up and go take a shower, I'ma end up right back on top of you."

"I won't stop you," Justina teased, circling Amir's nipple with the tip of her tongue.

"Damn, baby, you're making my dick hard again."

"That's a good thing." Justina grinned seductively.

"Not when I'm already running late," Amir said, kissing Justina one last time before getting out the bed.

"Babe, get back in bed."

"I have to meet Nico. If I'm late, he'll bring up that shit all day. He petty when it comes to shit like that," Amir joked.

"I feel you."

"I promise, I'll be back as soon as possible and I'ma turn that frown into a smile."

"You better!" Justina called out as Amir stepped into the shower. "That was some amazing sex." Justina began smiling while her naked body glided on the silk sheets. She was already anticipating Amir's return as her sex drive was insatiable. Right when Justina decided to pleasure herself since Amir wasn't available, she saw Desmond was calling her. She grabbed her cell phone and went outside on the balcony. "Desmond, hi."

"Hey, did you get my message?"

"I did. I was meaning to call you back, but my boyfriend's in town."

"I see, is he there now?"

"He's in the shower. I planned on calling you once he left."

"Then why did you answer the phone?"

"I wanted to hear your voice," Justina professed.

"I hadn't spoken to you since the night of the explosion. I wanted to make sure you were feeling okay."

"Does that mean you were concerned about my wellbeing, Mr. Blackwell?"

"No doubt. I'm not gonna keep you though. I'll let you get back to yo' man. Bye."

"Wait!' Justina yelled out, but Desmond had already hung up. She was tempted to call him back, but she knew Amir would be coming out the bathroom at any moment. But there was no denying, Justina wanted Desmond and for her it was more than lust, she wanted him to be her man.

Taren had spent her entire day on the phone trying to track down Dominique. She pretended to be everything from her sister, auntie, mother, even grandmother and kept coming up short. There wasn't a hospital or a morgue that had any record of a Dominique.

"Maybe the bitch is dead," Taren folded her hands on top of her head and said. She wanted to believe that to be true, but Taren couldn't risk it. So far she had gotten away with multiple murders, which didn't include the twenty people that died in the explosion and so many more that were injured. But it would only take one person to bring Taren's reign of terror to an abrupt end and she refused to let that happen.

"How you holding up?" Supreme asked Aaliyah who was sitting down in the Mediation Chapel, staring up at the stained glass window that depicted a calming nature scene. His hands rested on Aaliyah's shoulders and he could sense the stress consuming her body and spirit.

"I thought I would come in here and know exactly what to pray for. God would hear me and just like that Dale would wake up, all would be fine."

"Prayer is good. God is always listening, just speak to him." Supreme tried to encourage Aaliyah to do so.

"I attempted, but every time the words would start to come out, I thought about how much angrier I would be if God wasn't listening and Dale didn't get better."

"That's where faith comes in. This family has been through so much, yet we continue to rise. Clearly, our prayers are being heard. Don't be your own worst enemy," Supreme warned.

"You're right. You're so, so right." Aaliyah nodded her head in agreement. "I've gotten away with so much. I guess I didn't think I deserved any more favors. Although the favor is technically for Dale, it's really for me," she said glancing up at her father. "Daddy, I finally feel like I've found the perfect man for me and I don't want to lose him."

"Then you have to believe that you won't. I've been where you are. I thought I was gonna lose your mother, a few times actually," Supreme gave a slight chuckle. "But I never gave up hope, except for one time. I allowed Maya to take my mind to a very dark place and I'll always regret that. Don't make the same mistake I did."

"I won't!" Aaliyah now had a sparkle in her eyes as if she had been given a brand new understanding of life and love. "I adore you, Daddy. Thank you!" Aaliyah beamed, hugging her father tightly.

Chapter Eight

Fake Love

"Nico Carter, it's a pleasure to meet you." Desmond gave him a firm shake when he entered his office.

"Thank you. This is a business associate of mine," he said introducing Amir, "And he's family," Nico added.

"Nice to meet you, Amir." Both men shook hands. "I can't believe I have the legendary Nico Carter standing in my office. After all these years, you and your partner, Genesis, still hold a lot of clout in these streets. That's commendable," Desmond stated.

"Amir here is actually Genesis's son."

"Really? Wow, you have some big shoes to fill. You ready for that?"

"I'm not worried. My father's been preparing me for this all my life," Amir replied without hesitation."

"Yes, he has," Nico said proudly, patting Amir's shoulder. "We're all impressed with how you've been conducting business. But we're not here to boast on Amir," Nico joked.

"I don't mind." Amir smiled.

"I'm sure you don't." Nico eyed him. "But like I told you on the phone, I'm here to discuss that bomb that went off in your club. Both of my daughters could've died, so I'm takin' this shit personally."

"Mr. Carter..."

"Call me Nico."

"Nico, I had no idea Angel was your daughter. I'm not sure if she's told you, but we're partners in Angel's Girls," Desmond let him know.

"I didn't know that. Glad you told me, so I can make sure you're treating my daughter right."

"I'm above board when it comes to business. I have a great deal of respect for Angel. You have no need to worry."

"Good. Let's sit down and discuss why I wanted

to see you." Once they were seated and comfortable, Nico continued. "I have one of my men investigating who's responsible for setting off that bomb. I brought you a copy of some video he got for me that might be helpful."

"Impressive," Desmond said taking the disc from Nico and putting it in his laptop. "I was told there wasn't any video. Obviously, your investigator is better than mine." Desmond leaned back in his chair waiting for the video to load, feeling some type of way.

"Lucky for you, I don't mind sharing the information since we both want the same thing. As you can see there are two women entering the club using that side door. It doesn't show their faces, but you get a very clear back view and at one point a clear side view of one of the women. I was thinking maybe they worked at your club." Nico waited for Desmond to give a response.

Amir and Nico observed as Desmond scrutinized the video. His face was close up on the screen and he kept rewinding a certain part over and over. He had to watch at least ten times before saying a word.

"I don't recognize the woman with the hat on. And when she came back out the building she kept her head down the entire time as if she knew someone might be watching. But the woman with her, I swear that's Dominque," Desmond said with certainty.

"Dominique... where have I heard that name at?" Nico asked himself out loud.

"I wouldn't know, but she did work at my club. She was one of our new dancers."

"Would she have any reason to want to blow up your club?" Amir asked.

"No!" Desmond stated decisively. "Dominique is a sweet girl. She would never be caught up in anything like that."

"Have you spoken to her since the explosion? Was she one of the survivors?" Amir kept the questions going since Nico seemed preoccupied.

"She went missing about a week before the explosion. I had one of my men on it, but he couldn't locate her. It was like she vanished. I was concerned because a couple ladies from Angel's Girls had been murdered recently. I was beginning to think Dominique might be the latest victim. It's crazy seeing her on this video."

"Desmond, are you sure it's her?"

"Positive. When I saw the petite frame, I immediately thought of Dominique, but when I kept rewinding the frame showing the side of her face, there's not a doubt in my mind."

"Angel was trying to track down a young lady with the name Dominique. That's why she sounds familiar!" Nico announced suddenly.

"Why would Angel be tracking down Dominique? She didn't work for Angel's Girls only my nightclub." Desmond was puzzled.

"Angel said that she found Dominique knocked out and unconscious near the bomb before it exploded. She pulled the girl out, but the bomb went off before they were able to get out," Nico explained. "From my understanding, she did gain consciousness for a minute and that's when she told Angel her name, but soon after she lost consciousness again. After Angel went and helped Aaliyah and Justina she's not sure what happened to the young lady."

"So, for all we know, Dominique died in the explosion," Desmond bawled, slamming down the screen of his laptop. "I'm the one that brought Dominique to Miami. She was from some small town right outside Alabama. I promised her a better life; that all her dreams would come true. Instead she was left to die in my club," he seethed.

"Then her death can't be in vain," Nico said. "We have to find the other woman in the video because that's her killer and the person responsible for all the other deaths in that explosion. I am going to have Angel look at the footage to confirm it's the same Dominique she tried to save."

"I'm sure it is. I don't believe in coincidences. But I do want to find Dominique's killer. I owe her that. And when I do, she's dead," Desmond promised.

"I feel like I haven't seen you in forever." Aaliyah smiled, sitting across Justina at the Thai restaurant.

"I know. I was so surprised when you called and said you wanted to meet for lunch. You haven't left Dale's side in weeks."

"Yeah. After a lot of soul searching, I felt it was time for me to find a balance. You know, being there for Dale and not losing myself."

"Soul searching... that isn't really your style," Justina remarked.

"I guess I have my father to thank for that."

"Which one?"

"Supreme. We had a heart to heart and I have a brand new outlook about things."

"I'm happy for you." Justina smiled widely, lying through her teeth. *Aaliyah, it doesn't matter if Dale never gains consciousness or if he wakes up, you lose either way. You're so desperate for him to open his eyes but if he does, you'll be the last face he'll want to see,* Justina laughed to herself. She was feeling especially giddy because before the bomb went off, she received a text from Nesa telling her the job was done and Dale knew it was Supreme who killed his brother Emory. That's why when she noticed Nesa in the corner alive and needing help, Justina left her to die since she was no longer of any use to her.

"Walking around depressed isn't going to bring Dale back to me any sooner, but when he does wake up," Aaliyah perked up as if confident it would happen. "I want to be at my best," she smiled admiring her freshly done Haute Couture manicure.

"Aaliyah, I must admit, I was really concerned about your well being. You totally weren't yourself, but I see now you're back."

"Not a hundred percent, but your girl is on a comeback!" Aaliyah raised her hand and the ladies high-fived each other.

"I'm proud of you. You've taken a devastating situation and you're handling it with such courage. I truly admire you, Aaliyah."

"Thank you. That means a lot to me, Justina. I know our friendship has endured a tremendous amount of ups and downs."

"That's putting it mildly," Justina said laughing.

"True, but the point is, we've made it through it and we're closer than ever. And the fact that you admire me is really sweet."

Of course you think it's sweet, Aaliyah. You expect and want all of us to admire you. Heaven forbid everyone in the world doesn't bow down and think you're the most amazing girl in the world. Gosh, can you be any more self absorbed, Justina thought to herself.

"I've always admired you, Aaliyah. Even when we weren't on good terms. I think you're an exceptional person."

"You'll get no argument from me! But seriously, I'm starving. I'm gonna order something really yummy," Aaliyah said opening the menu. "Plus, I really need to gain back those few pounds I've dropped recently because my jeans aren't quite fitting the same."

"I'm pretty hungry myself." Justina browsed through the menu while twirling around the stirrer straw in her cocktail. "I think I know what I'm getting, what about you?"

"Hold on one second," Aaliyah said reaching for her phone. "This is the hospital calling me. "Hello."

Justina sat back in her seat hoping they were calling to tell her that Dale was dead. She knew how devastated Aaliyah would be. Then she quickly changed her mind. Justina decided it would be much more traumatic for Aaliyah if Dale woke up and hated her instead.

"What did the hospital say?" Justina asked.

"Omigosh, Dale is awake. I have to go!" Aaliyah appeared to be stunned, like she couldn't believe what she heard on the phone.

"Are you okay to drive... do you want me to come with you?"

"I know I must seem a lil' out of it, but I'm fine. I'll call you later on." Aaliyah went over and gave Justina a quick hug.

"Okay! I'm so happy Dale is awake and you're about to get everything you deserve." Justina blew Aaliyah what was equivalent to a kiss of death.

Chapter Nine

Chess Moves

Taren stepped on the elevator at the hospital, on her way up to visit with Angel. She wasn't looking forward to spending time with her former BFF, but Taren wanted to see if Angel had any news regarding Dominique since she was coming up short.

"Damn, maybe I should've taken the stairs," Taren mumbled in a low tone, annoyed the elevator seemed to be stopping on every floor. It was getting more and more crowded which irritated Taren even more since she was stuck in the back.

"Excuse me." A heavyset man grumbled, practically squishing Taren's arm.

"If this mutherfucker..." Taren bit down on her lip ready to explode. It was only five more levels up until she reached her floor so she contained herself. She heard the door open again, but kept her head down deciding not to look back up until it was time to get off.

"Let me move over for you," a man said when a nurse got on the elevator with a woman in a wheelchair.

"Thank you." The nurse smiled.

After the door opened and closed a couple more times, Taren glanced up to see how much longer she had to go. That's when she saw her; the nurse was pushing Dominique in a wheelchair off the elevator.

"Excuse me!" Taren yelled, trying to get off the elevator, but the heavyset man was blocking her way. She shoved his arm as hard as she could but once she made it past him, she had to get through a few more people in front of her. "Fuck!" she screamed when the doors closed in her face. Taren kept pushing down hard on the open door button but it was too late. The elevator kept going and didn't stop until it got to the floor Angel was on.

Taren was the first person off the elevator when the door opened. Instead of waiting for another elevator going down she opted for the stairs. "Can you tell me where the stairs are?" she asked an orderly.

"Straight down the hall and you'll see an exit sign." The man pointed.

"Thanks!" Taren headed in the direction the orderly pointed. She didn't want to run and bring unwanted attention to herself, but she was walking fast as hell, almost jogging. As Taren got closer to the exit she picked up her speed.

"Taren!" she heard someone call out.

Taren was tempted to keep going, but the voice got louder and she could tell people who were passing by her were looking at her like, 'Bitch, you don't hear somebody calling you.'

"Taren! You passed my room!" Angel called out.

"Fuck!" Taren's faced frowned down, but she turned around wearing a smile. "Oh, wow. How dumb am I?" She tapped her forehead as she got closer to Angel. "Girl, you know how forgetful I can be."

"Lucky for you I was seeing my dad off then I noticed you hauling ass down the hallway."

"Yeah, lucky for me." She laughed as they walked back to Angel's room. "So how much longer before you get to go home?"

"My doctor finally gave me clearance to leave tomorrow. I'm beyond thrilled. I'm starting to feel like a prisoner. I wish you had come a few minutes earlier. I really wanted you to meet my dad."

"That would've been nice."

"Yeah, I would call and tell him to come back, but he was in a rush. He finally found out who Dominique is," Angel revealed excitedly.

"Wow, that's awesome! Did he locate her?" Taren inquired, thinking she was gonna be sick.

"Unfortunately, not yet, but we're making progress. He stopped by to show me some video footage that a private investigator he hired had from the night of the explosion."

"This is getting better and better. What was on the video," Taren questioned, doing her best not to stutter due to her jumpiness. Only thing she wanted to do was go down to the floor Dominique was on and get rid of her for good.

"Right! He met Desmond."

"Your business partner?" Taren asked like she didn't already know the answer.

"Yeah, and you know he also owns Diamonds & Pearls."

"Duh!... I'm having a blonde moment," Taren joked.

"My dad showed Desmond first and he recognized the woman on the video as Dominique because she was a dancer at his club. My dad remembered that I was looking for a woman with that name, but he wanted to show me the video to make sure the two women were one and the same."

"That's crazy!"

"It's crazy and amazing. Now we have Dominque's full name and my dad is determined to find her. But there is a chance she's dead." Angel's eyes filled with sadness. "I'm praying she's not, but at least now we can contact her family if it comes to that."

"For your sake, I hope she's alive, but I hate to say it, for some reason I think Dominique's dead." That was wishful thinking mixed with some plotting on Taren's part.

"I would love to disagree with you, but I'm sorta feeling the same way. If she is dead then we've lost the only person who can identify the bomber because on the video you can't see the other woman's face."

"Really." Taren nodded, fidgeting with her dainty rose and gold anklet that was adorned with butterflies. Taren's anxiety was about to make her rip it right off her ankle. "You definitely need this Dominique woman to be found alive then."

"My father's private investigator is top notch. If Dominique's alive, he'll find her."

"I hate to leave so soon but maintenance is stopping by my apartment to fix a plumbing issue. I don't won't them to be in my apartment without me," Taren explained.

"Oh, no problem. Glad you were able to stop by," Angel said while Taren was giving her a hug.

"I'll call and check on you tomorrow. Once you're back home and settled in, we must plan to do lunch or dinner soon."

"For sure! Talk to you soon."

Taren waved bye to Angel and headed straight to the stairway. She had no clue how she was planning to kill Dominique. What Taren was sure of, Dominique wouldn't be leaving the hospital alive.

Justina was lounging in a nude reptile bikini at her condo complex as the hot sun radiated on her glistening skin. With the cool breeze circulating through the air, it was the perfect day to be lounging by the pool. Wearing her oversized, metallic frame, gold and pink sunglasses, sipping on a glass of wine while listening to music through her earpiece, Justina didn't even notice when Nesa walked up on her, until she felt the woman's cold hands.

"Who in the fuck are you?!" Justina snapped, removing her sunglasses before quickly recognizing the statuesque woman's face. "Oh, it's you. You're a lot taller than I remember," she mocked. What do you want and why are you here?"

"Is that how you talk to the woman who did yo' dirty work for you? Hmmm. Show some respect," Nesa smacked.

"I did show you respect, when I gave you all that money," she retorted with unapologetic arrogance. "You were supposed to take it and be gone. Again, I have to ask what are you doing here?"

"You one of those rich bitch snobs, ain't you?" Nesa smirked, sizing Justina up. "You laying there thinking you cute, living over here in this fabulous condominium like you hot shit and..."

"Do you have a point to make?" Justina scoffed cutting Nesa off. "If so, make it, if not then be gone. As you can see, I'm trying to enjoy the beautiful weather and you're blocking the sun."

"I guess you think you can dismiss me now because you don't need me. Is that why you left me for dead at that club?"

"I don't know what you're talking about." Justina placed her sunglasses back over her eyes like Nesa was nonexistent.

"You can try and ignore me all you like, but I ain't going nowhere. I asked yo ass to help me, but instead you walked away. If it wasn't for that woman Angel, I would be dead right now."

Justina continued to carry on, disregarding Nesa.

"The funny part is earlier that night Angel

71

came up to me after she saw me talking to Dale. She wanted to know what I said to him because he stormed off madder than a motherfucker. I asked why the fuck did she care. Come to find out, she's Aaliyah's sister. Nothing like that sisterly love." Nesa mischievously laughed.

"What do you want, Nesa!"

"I guess I have your attention now... huh? Good 'cause I'ma need some more money. With the club closed a bitch is broke."

"I gave you plenty of money to relocate. I even gave you a connect to another club in another state you could work at," Justina spit.

"I've decided I don't wanna leave Miami. When I survived my near death experience, I realized this is the only city for me. But if you don't want to pay up, I'm sure Angel would be more than happy to compensate me for the information I have. What do you think?"

"I think you're trying to blackmail me," Justina asserted.

"How about we call it one scandalous heifer looking out for another. You know us ladies have to stick together."

"How much do you want?"

"Think of a number that makes you uncomfortable and then double it." Nesa gave Justina a wicked smile.

"Fine. I'll call you tomorrow and let you know when you can pick your money up. Now leave."

"You better have my money tomorrow and don't try no sneaky shit 'cause I don't mind gettin' down and dirty in the mud."

"Neither do I," Justina warned. "I'll be in touch tomorrow." Justina laid back down, allowing the sun to energize her body now that Nesa was no longer blocking it. She had kept her cool, but Justina was incensed that Nesa had turned the tables on her. "If only that do-gooder Angel had minded her business and let Nesa die in that building," she fumed.

It was one thing for Justina to make chess moves, but she wasn't about to allow a chick she felt was beneath her enter the game as an equal playing partner. Nesa's bold demands had now moved her up to the top of Justina's hit list.

Chapter Ten

Wild Thoughts

"Baby, I know it's been a couple days, but I can't get over that your eyes are open, you're talking and eating." Aaliyah laughed, while Dale stuffed his face with hospital food like they were dining at a five-star restaurant. "Is it good?"

"Yo, right now this chicken sandwich taste like a prime steak. I guess being deprived of a decent meal for a couple weeks will do that to you."

"Before you know it, we'll be back at Prime 112

and you will be devouring a juicy steak."

"That's the first place we're going when I get out this joint."

"I'm down. You know how much I love their soy-marinated sea bass. Now you got me gettin' hungry talkin' about that place," Aaliyah quipped.

"Maybe we should have them cater our wedding," Dale suggested. Aaliyah stared at Dale without saying anything. "You know Emory love steak too and since he gon' be my best man, we gotta make sure he's straight." Dale nodded his head and grinned. "Why you so quiet... what you think?"

"I think it would be perfect." Aaliyah went and sat down next to Dale. "I'm surprised you're talking about our wedding so soon."

"Why wouldn't I? When I would hear niggas say this shit I thought they was mad corny. But now that I've experienced this, to me it's the realist shit ever."

"What's that?"

"Life is way too short to waste time, so live life to the fullest. I almost died, but I didn't. The quicker things go back to what they used to be, the sooner I can forget I was ever confined to this hospital bed."

"Are you hoping you can remember what happened the night when the bomb exploded or do you want to forget that too?"

"Hell no! I don't wanna remember that shit. I pray that night forever remains a blur for me," Dale scoffed. He grabbed the remote control, pressing down hard on the button to turn the channel, like he was trying to release his anger on the remote.

"Babe, I'll be right back. I'ma get a drink from the vending machine. Do you want anything?'

"No, I'm good," Dale answered not looking up.

Aaliyah left out his hospital room not for a drink, but to search for Dale's doctor. "Excuse me, Dr. Henderson!" she called out, waving her hand when she spotted him turning down the hallway. Aaliyah sprinted in his direction and was breathing heavily when she finally caught up with him. "Dr. Henderson!"

"Are you okay?" The doctor gave Aaliyah a peculiar stare, due to her bending over, huffing and puffing

"I'm fine," Aaliyah wheezed. The doctor continued with the peculiar stare. "I wanted to speak with you about my fiancé, Dale." She finally got her breathing under control and made a mental note to start back exercising ASAP.

"What about Dale?"

"I know you said it's common for patients to have no recollection when something traumatic happens, but how long does that typically last?" Aaliyah wanted to know.

"It varies from person to person." The doctor replied.

"What about in Dale's case?"

"I'm not sure. But his overall health appears to be fine so there is no reason for concern." The doctor smiled politely and began to walk away.

"Dr. Henderson, wait!" Aaliyah placed her hand on his shoulder. "Dale wants us to move forward on our wedding date, but is that really a good idea under the circumstances?"

"Unless the wedding is tomorrow, I don't think it should be a problem. Now, if you'll excuse me, I really..."

"Doctor," Aaliyah cut him off. "Not only does Dale not remember the night of the explosion, he made a comment about his brother being the best man at our wedding."

"What's the problem with that?"

"His brother, Emory, is dead."

"I see. When someone suffers head trauma, it's not uncommon for there to be gaps in their memory. Dale might speak of his brother being alive today, but tomorrow he could very well remember his brother is dead. I wouldn't be alarmed."

"Is it possible that would happen with me? Today Dale wants us to get married. A week from now could he forget he ever loved me?" Aaliyah sounded rattled.

"Don't panic." Dr. Henderson held Aaliyah's hand trying to reassure her. "I don't think you have anything to worry about, but I'll run some more tests. The most important thing is for you to be there for your fiancé and don't cause him or yourself any unnecessary stress. Do you think you can do that?" he questioned giving Aaliyah a warm smile.

"Yeah, I think I can handle that. Thank you so much, Dr. Henderson. I apologize if I came across as some neurotic woman. But I've finally found the man I want to spend the rest of my life with and I've been dreaming about our perfect wedding and I guess I'm scared it's gonna blow up in my face."

"No worries. It's perfectly normal. Now, I really must be going. Try to relax," he said heading off to see his next patient.

Aaliyah leaned back against the wall and stared out the window across from her. The afternoon storm was dispersing with the sun now peeping through the clouds. The vision was a depiction of Aaliyah's current mood. She believed the storm had passed and her life with Dale would be picture perfect.

"Yes, I'm here to deliver these flowers for Dominique Alston."

"Are you a relative? You can just take the flowers to her room," the lady at the front desk said. The problem was Taren had no idea what room Dominique was in. After doing a test run on another floor she knew they wouldn't give her that information. Now Taren was using a different approach on the floor she believed Dominique's room was actually on.

"No, I'm not a relative. I'm a carrier, simply delivering the flowers. Would you like me to take them to her room?" Taren offered.

"No. We'll take care of it. Thank you," the lady said then went back to what she was doing.

Taren headed towards the elevator before lingering off to the side waiting for the woman to make her move. She checked the card on the flowers for the name and appeared to be looking through something. Taren figured she was trying to verify Dominique's room number. The woman picked up the phone, chatted on it briefly and hung up. She then picked up the vase full of flowers and placed it behind the desk.

What the fuck is this stupid woman doing? Just take the damn flowers to Dominique's room so I can do what I have to do and get the hell outta here! Taren said to herself gradually becoming agitated.

Ten minutes, twenty minutes, and then thirty minutes passed with no movement. The flowers remained behind the desk and the woman was carrying on as if no flower delivery had been made. By this time, Taren wanted to run up on her and beat the woman down, but she continued to linger hoping to catch a break.

Almost an hour later, Taren noticed the nurse she had seen hours earlier getting off the elevator and she was still pushing Dominique.

"Hey!" the lady at the front desk stopped the nurse and said. "These flowers were delivered to your patient."

"These are beautiful. Dominique's not feeling well. I had to give her some medicine while we were in therapy so she's out of it. I'm going to get her settled in her room and I'll come back and get the flowers," the nurse said.

"Okay, they'll be right here."

From a slight distance, Taren followed behind the nurse while she pushed a sleeping Dominique in her wheelchair. When they stopped in front of the hospital room, Taren backed up and waited patiently for the nurse to come out so she could go in. She knew there would be a small window of time for her to go in, kill Dominique, and get out without detection. Every second counted and Taren planned to use her time wisely.

"About damn time," Taren mumbled when the nurse exited out the room fifteen minutes later and headed back to the front desk. "Perfect." She smiled when the nurse stopped in the hallway to speak to someone. They seemed to be having a deep discussion, which Taren welcomed. That gave her more time to tend to Dominique.

Taren was wearing a baseball cap and had it pulled down low over her eyes. She walked slowly but with purpose. *Once I get rid of Dominique, I can finally end Angel. I swear that girl seems impossible to kill,* Taren thought to herself as she was about to enter Dominique's room. But that arrogant grin vanished from Taren's face when she was greeted with an unexpected guest.

"So sorry. I must have the wrong room," Taren said when she saw two hulking men, dressed in black, posted inside Dominique's room. She was so scared and taken off guard that Taren didn't even look up to make eye contact with the men. She wanted to get out before they had an opportunity to grill her ass.

I'm fucked! Taren mouthed, damn near tripping, coming out the room. She had no clue what to do next. Dominique now had guards, which meant she had been found and was being protected. She knew it was only a matter of time before the secret was out and her cover would be blown. The clock was ticking and Taren had to make a move fast.

Chapter Eleven

Lust On The Brain

"I have two men guarding Dominque. I got them niggas in her room. The only time they step out is when the doctor or nurse need privacy. Even then, they posted right there," Miles told Desmond.

"It better stay like that, 'cause I don't want any fuckups. Make sure Dominique is comfortable and she has everything she needs," Desmond stressed.

"Got you. I know she's important to you."

"Yeah, she is. I also don't want anybody asking

Dominique no questions until I speak to her first. Somebody took down my club. That means they targeting me. I wanna be the one to hand out retribution," Desmond made clear. "I can't make that happen until I speak to Dominique. When do you think that will be?"

"I spoke to her nurse and she's not sure. There's some different issues going on with Dominique so she's heavily medicated. She doesn't think Dominique will be lucid enough to give you any credible info until they lower her dosage."

"When will that be?" Desmond pressed, but Miles shrugged his shoulders. "You don't think this nurse is feeding you bullshit so she can stay on the payroll longer?"

"Nah," Miles was quick to say. "When we finally located Dominique and I went to her with my proposition, I hit her off lovely. She knows she doesn't get the remainder of her payment until after you speak to Dominique. So, she wants her to get better. The sooner she does, the sooner she gets paid," Miles explained.

"Cool. Make sure you monitor the situation. The nurse does understand that Dominique is to have no visitors?"

"Mos def!" Miles shook his head.

"Good, because I'm positive Nico has his private investigator on it. If he knew Dominique was right there in the same hospital as Angel, he would try to have the whole place shut down... trust me."

"Luckily, we got the break first," Miles stated. "How was it meeting the great Nico Carter anyway? Does he measure up to the street legend hype that's followed him for years?"

"I would say yes. He has that presence about him."

"You mean arrogance?" Miles laughed.

"Actually not. I guess he's too confident in his capabilities to be arrogant," Desmond said, stepping behind his desk to look at his phone.

"Sounds like you," Miles commented.

"Haven't gotten to that level yet. Yeah, I'm confident but the arrogance ain't left yet," Desmond joked, eyeing his phone and noticing he had two missed calls from Justina. "I think we've covered everything," he said ready to wrap up his conversation with Miles so he could call Justina back.

"Cool. If I get any news regarding Dominique, I'll hit you up. Oh yeah, you never told me which location for the club you decided to go with," Miles said right before he was heading out.

"I'm going with the prime location right there on South Beach."

"Wise decision." Miles winked.

"I think so too. The good news is, it used to be a club already. Very high end, top-notch equipment;

décor on point. It was only open for a couple months before for the dude who owned it got locked up by the Feds. He had to start unloading shit and one of those things was that club. His unfortunate predicament ended up being a lucky gain for me," Desmond stated.

"Lucky indeed. You got an opening date yet?"

"If everything continues to go smoothly, in about three weeks. I'm going real big with this. I'm locking down an A-list performer and all proceeds from opening night is going to be donated to the families of the victims from the explosion."

"Nice." Miles was highly impressed.

"What happened was a tragedy, but I have to find some kinda way to put a positive spin on it. If I don't, people will always associate Diamonds & Pearls to what happened that night. I don't want that."

"It's understandable. I know all the hard work you put into that club. You're a legitimate business-man now. You don't want that to be tainted."

"I don't and it shouldn't be. I blame the person who set off that bomb in my club for the legacy I'm trying to build to even be in jeopardy. Whoever they are, hope they know their days are numbered," Desmond promised.

Justina stared at her phone seething. "Why the fuck didn't you answer my calls!" she yelled out loud. She tried to resist but Justina had been unable to get Desmond off her mind. When she finally broke down and called him, her ego took a hit when he didn't answer. Not wanting to come across as desperate and needy, it was taking all of Justina's self control not to blow up his phone. "Fuck it!" she spit, reaching for her cell to try one more time, but this time she was interrupted.

"Hey, babe." Amir smiled when he came into the bedroom.

"Hey, my love," Justina hugged and kissed Amir. "I didn't hear you come in. How was your day?"

"It was busy. Running around with Nico again all day. I had no idea he handled the amount of business he did in Miami. He said he could use my help out here."

"Does that mean you're thinking about staying for a while?" Justina questioned.

"I wish I could, if only to spend some more time with you, but I'm needed back in New York tonight. My dad is still out of the country with my mom. Lorenzo is in LA with Dior, of course Nico is here.

Our main headquarters is NYC so I have to tend to it."

"I wish I could go back with you," Justina whined, wrapping her arms around Amir's neck.

"Aaliyah has a lot going on right now. It's good you're staying here with her. Nico said the wedding is moving forward as scheduled so after that you can ditch Miami and come back to yo' man." Amir pulled Justina in close kissing her.

"I can't wait. Have you seen Aaliyah since Dale came out of his coma?"

"No, but we spoke on the phone a few times. She's been in the hospital with him day and night. When I spoke to her earlier she said they're discharging him in a few days."

"Aaliyah must be thrilled."

"You know it." Amir grinned, getting his belongings together. "I'm surprised you ain't spoke to her."

"We talked briefly yesterday, but like you said she's been glued to Dale's side. I'm trying to give her space so they can reconnect. It's so crazy how he doesn't remember anything from that night."

"Yeah, head trauma is tricky. Dale even made a comment to Aaliyah about his brother Emory."

"What sort of comment?"

"I can't remember the exact words but something to the effect that Emory was alive."

"Dale doesn't know his brother is dead?"

"Nope. At least a few days ago he didn't."

"Who killed Emory anyway?" Justina casually asked.

"I have no idea," Amir lied. There was no doubt in Justina's mind that Amir knew it was Supreme who killed Emory. It made her skin crawl that he could look her in the face and without hesitation lie to her.

"I see."

"The point is Emory is dead. For Aaliyah's peace of mind, hopefully Dale will remember that so she doesn't have to be the one to break the news to him." Amir sighed.

"I agree and hopefully when he remembers his brother is dead, he'll also remember everything that happened the night of the explosion."

"Maybe he will, maybe he won't. Remembering that night isn't necessary, but his brother being dead is because he ain't coming back," Amir said grabbing his tote bag. "I gotta go but make sure you look after Aaliyah."

"You know I will," Justina said sweetly.

"If time permits, I'll be back in a couple weeks. If not, I'll be here for the wedding."

"Okay, baby. Do you want me to take you to the airport?"

"No. A car is downstairs waiting for me. I'll call

you later on when I get back to New York," Amir said giving Justina a kiss.

"I don't want you to go. Let me feel you inside me one more time since I'll have to wait for so long." Justina glided her hand across Amir's chiseled face.

"I wish I could, babe, but I have to make this flight," Amir said ready to give into temptation. "Damn, if you kiss me there one more time, I ain't gonna make it to the airport on time." Amir closed his eyes becoming aroused as the tip of Justina's tongue danced around his neck.

"I know you want me," she whispered in Amir's ear with her hand pressed against his rising dick.

"Shit, you know I do," he moaned. "I gotta go, Justina." Amir finally contested once she started unzipping his pants. "I'll call you later. Love you!" he gave her a quick kiss and rushed out before she could make another move on him.

Justina threw herself down on the bed agitated that Amir was able to resist her. She wanted to use sex to control him, but it wasn't working. That gave her another excuse to prey on Desmond, but Justina knew she'd have to spin her web a little differently to lure him in. So, when Desmond finally returned her call, instead of answering, Justina sent him straight to voicemail.

Chapter Twelve

Deal Breakers

"Where you going?" Nesa's cousin, TJ, asked when he saw her in the bathroom getting all dolled up.

"To meet the chick I told you about that's gonna lace me wit' all that cash," Nesa bragged putting some highlighter on her cupid's bow.

"You gettin' awfully cute to go meet a bitch. You sure ya ain't fuckin'," TJ popped.

"Boy bye! I always try to look cute when I know I'm 'bout to get paid. 'Cause as soon as them coins hit my palms, I'm hittin' the mall. If you act right, you can come with, and I'll buy you something too," Nesa teased, blowing her cousin a kiss.

"Bitch, let me find out you 'bout to come into some serious cash. Yo' stingy ass must be seeing more than a couple zeros if you offering to let me buy something."

"Yep! She already hit me wit' some cash for a favor I did for her. I thought it was a come up for the little work I had to do until I decided to do a Google search on that ass."

"What did you find out?" TJ was dying to know.

"She's a rich bitch. Comes from long money, so my paper betta be right."

"How you know she's willing to share?"

"Because if she doesn't, I'll be spilling all her tea," Nesa quipped before putting on her Urban Decay finishing spray. "This shit here gon' have my makeup looking flawless all day," she said admiring herself in the mirror.

"Ooooooh, I can't wait to see how this unfold. Yo' tea must be juicy, 'cause rich fish don't normally like to share they coins wit' random bitches," TJ mocked.

"Don't underestimate yo' cuz. Have yo' phone handy because I'ma call you when I'm ready to hit the mall. Tootles!" Nesa waved enthusiastically as she was leaving, like she was about to cash in her lottery ticket.

Taren hadn't left her apartment since she discovered Dominique was being guarded as if she was under protection from the secret service. Chain smoking and blunts were no longer enough to subdue Taren's paranoia and anxiety. She was now lacing her weed with cocaine to take the edge off. She was expecting for the entire Miami Dade police department to come kicking down her front door at any minute.

"Oh, shit! It's Angel!" Taren's hand was shaking as she debated if she should answer. "Hello!" she shouted, not able to resist finding out if Angel now knew the truth.

"Taren, is that you?"

"Yeah, yeah. I had ran out and I was rushing back in to get my phone. I didn't even look to see who was calling." Taren went out on her balcony and lit up a cigarette. "So, what's up?" she asked nervously, waiting for Angel to start cursing her out.

"I've been home for a few days now and I'm finally settled in." There was this awkward silence, but Angel continued on. "I said I would call you so we could do lunch or dinner once everything was good with me."

"Right! Glad you home and feeling good. You

know I would love for us to hang out. What day you thinking?"

"What about tomorrow?" Angel asked.

"Tomorrow works," Taren said biting her nails.

"Great. Our usual spot?"

"You know it."

"Cool. I'll text you later on with the time. See you tomorrow!"

"Angel!" Taren called out before she could hang up.

"Huh?"

"Have you heard anything about the woman... I forget her name, you were looking for?"

"Oh, you're talking about Dominique."

"Yeah, that's her. Any word?" Taren pried.

"No," Angel sulked. "My dad had some leads, but he hasn't been able to find out any additional information. He's not giving up, but it's not looking good."

"So sorry to hear that. I'm keeping my fingers crossed for you."

"I appreciate that. I'll keep you posted if I do find out anything. Bye, girlie!"

Taren's head was spinning after getting off the phone with Angel. *If her father isn't the one who has those guards posted up in Dominique's room then who? It can't be the cops because those damn sure wasn't no police officers dressed in all black, looking like they could kill a nigga with one snap. But who would protect her like that and why are they keeping it from Angel?* Taren had so many questions in her head but no answers. It didn't change the fact Dominique could ID her and if she hadn't already she would very soon.

"Hello, there." Nesa greeted Justina with a smile when she came prancing over to the table at the low-key, somewhat rundown diner they agreed to meet at.

Justina wasted no time taking out the envelope from her purse. She put it on the table, placing her hand on top. "This is for you." Justina slid the envelope slightly forward. Nesa reached for it with excitement, but Justina quickly slid it back. "But before I give it to you."

"What, you wanna order some lunch. Let me take a look at the menu," Nesa smirked.

"Order whatever you like," Justina said playing with the diamond pendant around her neck. "But I'll pass. This place isn't really my style."

"Then why have us meet here?"

"Because it fits your style perfectly... don't you think?" Justina let out the most annoying giggle. It had Nesa ready to take her purse and smack her all across her head, but she wanted her money more.

"Let's get back to business. I have things to do," Nesa smacked.

"Take this money and forget you ever met me. This is a one-time warning," Justina made clear handing Nesa the envelope. Once that happened, Nesa had tuned her out. She was too busy counting the cash that she didn't hear another word Justina said.

"Hold the fuck up! Where the rest of my money?" Nesa scoffed, dropping the envelope.

"Excuse me? This is plenty. That's triple what I gave you just to have a conversation with Dale. A conversation, by the way, he has no recollection of due to the head injury he suffered in that explosion. I got absolutely nothing out the deal. So, I advise you to take all this easy money you've gotten, walk out that door, and don't look back."

"Listen you uppity bitch, I did what you hired me to do. It ain't my fault Dale don't remember shit. I'll be more than happy to tell him again, but it'll cost you."

Justina rolled her eyes, mad she made the mistake of hiring Nesa to do her dirty work.

"Furthermore, I know who yo' daddy is. T-Roc probably spends more on one of those fancy suits he be wearing than what's in this envelope."

"Leave my father out of this!" Justina barked.

"Did I get a rise outta yo' uptight ass?! Good, maybe now you know I mean business and I'm done playin' wit' you!" Nesa barked back.

"Don't push me."

"Or what?" Nesa folded her arms and twisted her neck hard, letting Justina know she had no plans of backing down. "Ain't nobody scared of you. Sweetheart, I'm from the gutter. I had to learn tricks and hustles in order to survive that a snotty brat like you could never even conceive. If you think what amounts to pocket change for a broad like you is gonna shut me up, then you don't know what type of bitch you dealing wit'."

"Oh, I know exactly what type of bitch I'm dealing with." Justina then reached back in her purse and pulled out a much larger envelope, tossing it at Nesa.

Nesa's eyes lit up staring at all the hundred dollar bills inside. "Now this more like it!" she beamed. "I knew you had it in you, girl! We might can be besties now," Nesa joked.

"I know your type. I'm well aware of how greedy women like you are."

"I'm not greedy, just smart," Nesa countered. "You act like you so sweet and innocent, but ain't nothing nice about you... you cold. I'm simply tryna get all I can out the deal."

"Of course you are, and it will never stop. You'll always want more."

"Not true, Justina. This right here is enough for me to get the hell outta Miami," Nesa said gleefully putting both envelopes in her purse. "I need some new dick to hustle anyway. As you can imagine, I've pretty much worn out my welcome here."

"I'm sure you have." Justina's eyes were shooting darts in Nesa's direction. "Who would've thought that a low budget stripper would be the one to put me in my place," she said in a condescending voice.

"I would offer to buy you lunch, but like you said, this place isn't your style. Plus, I've gotten everything I need and I have lots to do. Gotta go!" Nesa threw up the peace sign right after she adjusted the strap on her burgundy camisole, ready to strut out the diner and start spending her money. "By the way, be careful when you're leaving. I hear this is a very seedy neighborhood."

Nesa had left a frown on Justina's face, one that would easily turn permanent if she allowed her to have the upper hand. Justina was well aware that Nesa was rejoicing believing she had won and outsmarted her. That infuriated Justina more than handing over all that cash.

"You think you won this battle Nesa, but I'm fixated on winning the war," Justina seethed as she sent a text and then immediately deleted it.

Chapter Thirteen

Gone Wrong

"I got an update for you," Miles informed Desmond when he entered his office.

"I can speak with Dominique?"

"Not yet... but Sammie just called me and the dude Rico finally got back to him."

"Who the fuck is Rico?"

"He's the dude Clarissa mentioned Aspen was supposed to meet with before she got killed. You told Sammie to follow up with him," Miles reminded

Desmond.

"That's right. He's the one that does security work and was on the road with an artist."

"Yep. He's in town for a few days and Sammie is meeting with him Thursday to find out what information he might have, if any."

"I wanna be there. Sammie didn't even wanna follow up wit' dude. I don't trust him to ask the right questions."

"No problem. I'll find out from Sammie the time and place so you can speak to this Rico cat yo'self," Miles said.

"Good. If we can get some leads while we wait for Dominique to come around, then we need to. I gotta feeling speaking to Rico will prove to be extremely beneficial.

Nesa wasn't sure if she wanted to leave everything behind and head straight to the airport now to start a new life, or did she want to hit the mall first. "This what happens when a bitch got options!" Nesa began chanting, flinging the envelopes full of money she just collected from Justina while driving.

"Fuck it! Let me do a lil' shopping first so I can floss on these hoes before I leave Miami," Nesa said, calling her cousin.

"Did the rich fish come through?!" TJ screamed in the phone when he answered.

"Yes, motherfucker she did! I'm a rich bitch now," Nesa boasted loudly. "Get dressed. I'll be there in thirty minutes to pick you up. We going shopping. Bye!"

Nesa turned up her radio and started singing along to Rihanna on 'Wild Thoughts'. She envisioned herself recreating one of the looks from the video. While Nesa struggled with deciding if the dress Rihanna had worn was blue or green, so she could buy something similar, she didn't notice the dark sedan until it slammed into the back of her car.

"What an idiot!" Nesa yelled pulling over to the side of the street. At first she didn't want to get out because she was in a rough neighborhood, but her anger made her say fuck it. "You need to watch where you going," she popped, slamming her car door.

"My bad. I got a call... looked down, got distracted," the man explained.

"Hmm, whatever. You put a dent in the back of my car," Nesa snapped. "Give me all your information, including your insurance and driver's license, 'cause you have to fix this. Or I could call the police right now," Nesa threatened, reaching in her purse like she was going to make the call, although she had no desire to be bothered with the cops.

"How 'bout we avoid all that and I write you a check right now," he offered.

"I don't accept checks." Nesa sulked, placing her hands on her hips.

"Will cash do?"

"If you have enough of it," she countered.

"I believe I have enough to cover the damage. I'll get it for you."

Nesa glanced down at her watch, ready to go. The dent wasn't that bad and with the windfall of money she just came into she was tempted to fix it herself. But he fucked it up, so Nesa decided he should be the one to fix it.

"Could you hurry up. I have someplace I need to be!" she called out. Nesa looked around and it was the middle of the day, but there wasn't another face to see. She started feeling uneasy. "What's taking so long?" she questioned walking towards the man's car.

"One second. I'm counting the money," the man replied. He was reaching in his glove compartment when the sun flickered, showing a flash of metal. Nesa knew it was a gun. In that instance, she and the man's eyes locked. She turned to run back to her car, but the man reached out and grabbed her arm. Nesa began to scream out for help, but there was no one around to hear her. Not taking any chances the man swung his hand to cover Nesa's mouth. She bit down as hard as she could on his finger. Pissed off, he took his gun and knocked her on the side of the head. It caused Nesa to fall down on the concrete, scraping her knee.

"This nigga tryna kill me," she mumbled grabbing her head. Nesa knew she had to act fast because there wasn't a soul in sight to save her ass. Being a lady of the streets, she always kept some sort of protection on her, but her gun was in the car. So Nesa reached in her purse and grabbed her pepper spray. Before the man could pull the trigger and put a bullet in the back of Nesa's head, she unleashed her only available weapon. It wasn't a gun, but it was effective.

Immediately the man began coughing, choking. It dilated the capillaries of his eyes triggering temporary blindness, the mucous membranes swelled to the point of cutting off all but life support breathing, causing intense burning, making the man temporarily incapacitated. Nesa used his deteriorated condition to make a run to her car and haul ass.

"That bitch Justina tried to have me killed!" Nesa roared. Her heart rate had skyrocketed and she was sweating bullets, but Nesa was clear minded enough to know that what had just happened had Justina's name written all over it. "You done fucked up now," Nesa fumed, speeding off.

"I was pleasantly surprised when you called asking me to come over. How are you? You look great!" Justina said, kissing Aaliyah on the cheek.

"Thank you. I feel awesome." The sparkle that faded away while dealing with Dale's health scare was now back in full swing for Aaliyah. "Dale has improved at like rapid speed. Can you believe yesterday he actually wanted to take the car keys and drive himself around?"

"Wow, that's pretty amazing."

"And nerve wrecking," Aaliyah added. "It's wonderful he's getting better, but I'm like slow down. Seeing him in that hospital bed, not knowing if he would ever wake up was torture. I don't want him to do anything to jeopardize all the progress he's made. But Dale is so hardheaded." Aaliyah shrugged. "He's out running some errands now, but of course our driver is with him."

"With all the progress Dale is making has he remembered what happened the night of the explosion?" Justina asked.

"Not yet. But he does remember that Emory is dead which is a relief because I definitely didn't want to be the one to tell him."

"Yeah, I'm sure."

"But all of that is behind us and I'm focusing on our wedding. With everything that happened I thought maybe we should downsize how extravagant it's supposed to be, but Dale wasn't having it. He wants us to stick to our original plan."

"Aaliyah, I'm thrilled it's coming together for you. You and Dale deserve to be happy."

"Yeah, we do. I was even thinking about us starting a family immediately instead of waiting."

"Really?! Are you ready to be a mother? I mean raising a child is no joke. Ask our parents, I'm sure they would agree," Justina cracked.

"I bet they would, but I'm ready for the challenge. Sharing a beautiful baby with Dale would be the greatest gift ever. I think he would be an incredible dad," Aaliyah gushed. "Enough about my love life, how are things with you and Amir?"

"They're really good. It was nice we were able to spend some time together, even if it wasn't under the best circumstances."

"I spoke to him a few times while he was here and it's obvious you're making him happy."

"Why do you say that?" Justina questioned.

"Because he made me promise to keep an eye on you and make sure nobody steals you away while you're in Miami."

"Amir is so silly."

"I told him he had nothing to worry about because you only had eyes for him. Once the wedding is over you'll be back in New York with him."

"Exactly." That's what Justina's mouth said, but deep down she was yearning for something much different. She wanted to see where things could go between her and Desmond. Justina knew it would more than likely only be a temporary fling, mainly because she hadn't let go of her original goal which was to bring down not only Aaliyah but Amir too. She wanted to rip out his heart, stomp all over it and toss it to the side. So, he could feel the pain that he caused her after he and Aaliyah hooked up. Justina refused to deny herself a little bit of fun with Desmond in the meantime.

"In the end, things have worked out the way that they should. I'm marrying Dale and you ended up back with Amir. Too bad I didn't know that before me and Amir got together. I would've saved you a lot of heartache and all of our relationships such chaos," Aaliyah admitted with regret.

"We were young. Mistakes were made, but our lives are back on track. And like you said, it all worked out the way it should. Now you're getting married and I'm going to be your..." Justina became distracted and didn't finish her thought. "Aaliyah, hold on for one second. I really need to take this call," she said stepping out the room. "Why are you calling me?" Justina asked angrily.

"It's an emergency."

"It better be for you to be calling my fuckin' phone."

"It is. Meet me in our spot in one hour. Don't be late."

"Fine!" Justina ended the call furious. Within seconds Justina's phone started ringing again, but this time it was the last person she wanted to speak to. "Hello."

"Bitch, you tried to have me killed! I knew you were cold, but I didn't know yo' ass was bat shit crazy too!" Nesa yelled.

"Who is this?" Justina played dumb.

"Nah hoe, that shit ain't gon' work. You know who the fuck this is."

"Nesa, is that you?"

"Who tha fuck else would it be! You messed up doing that shit to me!"

"Nesa, I have no idea what you're talking about. You really should calm down."

"I'll calm down after I fuck yo' uppity ass up! Don't pretend you didn't send that nigga to kill me. Welllllllllll," Nesa took an extended pause before continuing. "The bitch is not dead and I'ma get that ass. So, watch yo' back, Justina, 'cause I'm comin' for you!"

Justina paced in the foyer for a few seconds, livid Nesa was still alive. "I knew I should've killed that hussy myself," she reeked. "If I wanna get something done, I always have to do it myself." She marched back into the sitting room.

"Are you okay?" Aaliyah questioned sensing something was wrong with her best friend. "You appear a tad bit frazzled."

"I was supposed to wire some money to my brother. He didn't want to ask our parents for it and I completely forgot. That was him calling me, spazzing out. I hate to run out on you, but I need to catch the bank before they close."

"No, go ahead. Trust me, I get it. Call me later so we can discuss all your maid of honor duties."

"I can't wait!" Justina gave one of her best fake smiles and left to deal with her Nesa situation.

Chapter Fourteen

Closer To The Truth

"Taren, you've barely touched your food. Normally, you would've devoured your calamari by now," Angel observed, especially since she was more than halfway done with her grilled salmon.

"I'm good. I just don't have much of an appetite."

"Since when? We've had our love of good food in common since elementary school," Angel cracked.

Taren took her fork and played with her food a little, not responding.

"You seem like you lost some weight too and your nail polish is chipped. I'm not trying to nitpick, but usually you're so together. If there's something going on, you know you can tell me, Taren. No matter what it is."

Taren put down her fork and then proceeded to wipe away one lonely tear streaming down her cheek.

"What's going on?" Angel reached across the table and held Taren's hand. "Please tell me what's wrong," she pleaded.

"I didn't wanna tell you this, but I need some time off from Angel's Girls."

"How much time do you need?"

"I'm not sure."

"Oh gosh, Taren, you're not sick are you?'

"No, nothing like that. It's..." Taren put her head down as if becoming choked up.

"It's what?!"

"My mother has hit rock bottom. A few months ago she was making so much progress. She had a new boyfriend, she got a little job. I thought she was gonna stay clean this time. But she broke up with her man, lost her job, which resulted into a major setback."

"Dear God." Angel shook her head in sorrow. "I'm so, so sorry, Taren. I still remember when we were little girls and we would watch your mom do her hair and makeup, then put on one of her pretty dresses. We thought she was so beautiful. Do you remember that?"

"I do, but she isn't that woman anymore. She hasn't been that woman for a very long time," Taren hated to say.

"So, are you going to stay with her? Do you think that will help? Maybe you should bring her here and let her live with you. A change of environment might be good for her," Angel suggested.

"I think you're absolutely right about a change of environment, but I really wanted to put her in the private rehab called Harmony Place in Malibu. I did some research and I think it would be perfect for my mom, but it's so expensive and I really can't afford it."

"Say no more," Angel said reaching in her purse and taking out her checkbook. "I believe this will be more than enough to cover your mom's rehab cost and your expenses while you take time off to get her situated."

"Angel, I can't ask you to do that!"

"You're not, I'm offering. Although, I wish you would've come to me."

"You've had so much going on, with the explosion and everything."

"I'm fine. I knew something had been bothering you and I feel like such a bad friend for not asking sooner. We're like family, Taren. You can come to me for anything. I love you like a sister."

"I love you too, Angel."

"Now take this," she said handing Taren the check. Her eyes widened in disbelief when she saw the amount it was written for.

"I don't know what to say. My mother will be able to have a long stay there." Taren smiled.

"If you need more let me know. I want your mother to heal and get better. Drug addiction is no joke. It's one of the hardest beasts to kill. Harmony Place is pricey, but I've heard it's worth every dollar."

"You have no idea how much this means to me. I can't wait to tell my mother I'm coming home and together we'll beat this addiction."

"That's a beautiful thing." Angel smiled.

"And it's all because of you," Taren returned the smile.

"I'm happy I can do it. I know what you're going through right now is hard on your mom, but it's also difficult for you. But at least you still have your mom. I never knew mine and my grandmother who did raise me, I would give everything I have to get her back, if only for a day. Once your mother gets clean you'll see what a blessing it is to have her in your life."

"I believe you're right, Angel."

"Do you know when you're leaving?"

"I'm going to get my belongings together and try to leave by the end of the week. I want to get to my mom as soon as possible. I don't want her to go off on some drug binge and disappear for a week," Taren said.

"I agree. The sooner you get to her the better. I'm going to miss you, girlie, but you're doing the right thing," Angel beamed.

"Thank you, Angel. This new journey I'm taking with my mom is all due to your generosity. I will forever be grateful." Taren got out of her chair and gave Angel a hug. I don't know what I would do without you."

Nesa ran into her apartment and immediately began packing up her shit, only taking what she considered necessities.

"Girl, what is wrong wit' you and why you look like somebody went upside yo' head?" TJ smacked. "I'm dressed and ready to hit the mall and you looking like that," he said frowning.

"I look like this because somebody did go upside my head," Nesa spit, pulling out the drawers on her dresser, grabbing stuff. "That trifling bitch tried to kill me!"

"You mean the rich fish?"

"Yes!"

"I knew she wasn't going to give up those coins voluntarily. I don't give a damn how much money she got," TJ said shaking his head. "What exactly did she do?"

"She sent some goon to hit me in the back of the car and when I got out he tried to shoot me."

"In broad daylight?! That bitch bold."

"I sprayed his ass with pepper spray."

"Yes, honey!" he said high fiving his cousin. "When I gave you that shit, I told you it would come in handy," TJ boasted proudly.

"It saved my life today, but I know that heifa ain't gon' give up. She probably know where I live. I can't stay here."

"Well, neither can I... shit! Where exactly are you going anyway?"

"A hotel."

"It better have double beds because I'm coming wit' you."

"Fine, but you need to hurry up. Now that I know what kinda chick I'm dealing wit', I don't feel safe here."

"Why don't you call the police?" TJ asked.

"And tell them what? This chick that I blackmailed sent somebody to kill me. I doubt they'd believe it, especially once they pull my criminal record."

"You gotta point there," he said nodding.

"Once I get out of this apartment, smoke me some weed, and have a couple shots of Hennessy, I'll be able to think. Once I figure out what to do, I'ma make sure Justina gets hers," Nesa swore.

"Desmond Blackwell, it's a pleasure to meet you man." Rico grinned hard as hell shaking Desmond's hand.

"Thanks for seeing me."

"Yo, if I had known this was for you, I woulda got back in touch a lot sooner. Ummm, no disrespect to you, man," he said looking over at Sammie who stood to the side with his face twisted up. "You are Desmond Blackwell. Man, that's messed up what happened to your club. Sorry about that."

"Thank you, but I'll be reopening in a few weeks."

"Word! If you need any security work, I'm yo' guy," Rico said.

"Give your information to Miles and I'll make something happen."

"Good looking out! I appreciate that." He shook Desmond's hand again.

"I don't have much time..."

"Of course," Rico jumped in and said. "I know you a busy man. So, you wanted to ask me about Aspen?"

"Yes. Clarissa said you met with Aspen because she had some questions for you regarding a young lady named Taren."

"That's correct. I used to be mad cool wit' this dude named Tony Marsh. He also worked in security."

"What did Tony Marsh have to do with Taren?"

"From what I remember, Aspen was trying to connect Tony with Taren because she believed they both had something to do with this girl getting killed."

"What girl?" Desmond asked.

"I can't remember the girl's name but she worked for the same company as Aspen."

"You must be talking about Laurie," Desmond reasoned. "Did Taren and this Tony dude know each other?"

"There was this chick I saw him with a few times when we would hang out. I couldn't remember her name but I did remember her face. Aspen was supposed to meet up with me again to bring a picture of the girl because she didn't have one on her, but she never showed up. Now I know it's because she got killed and shawty seemed cool too."

"Damn, I don't have no picture of Taren either,

but I know somebody who does. Rico, I need you to take a ride wit' me," Desmond told him. "Everybody let's go."

Desmond planned to get to the bottom of this shit today. He wanted to know what role, if any, Taren played in Laurie's death and if she had any other skeletons in her closet. If she did, Desmond was going to expose them all.

Chapter Fifteen

Gone Girl

"What the fuck is wrong with you, Dirk?! I give you a simple job to do and instead of delivering, you're standing there with this pathetic puppy dog stare on your face," Justina raged.

"How was I was supposed to know she carries pepper spray! I thought she had permanently blinded me."

"Do I look like I give a damn? You should've never given her chance to do any of that. How hard is it to pull the trigger and kill somebody! Now that lowlife hoe is alive and knows I'm the one behind the botched hit." Justina bit down on her bottom lip, contemplating what Nesa might do next.

"I know I fucked up, but I can make this shit right. Now that I know what type of broad I'm dealing wit', I'll be better prepared," Dirk said.

"I told you she was a two-dollar stripper. What else did you need to know?" Justina stared at him dumbfounded.

"She got some street edge wit' her. That mean she hip to shit... constantly sniffing out game. You gotta move quick wit' broads like that. Or they do shit like this, pepper spray a nigga. Luckily she ain't have no heat wit' her. I might be in the hospital right now or either dead. Come on, Justina, I'm good for it. Let me finish what I started," he implored.

"Fine, Dirk. I'ma give you forty-eight hours to kill that bitch. After that, if Nesa's not dead, I'm taking over. And don't call me, I'll get in touch with you." Justina put on her rose gold, oversized cat eye sunglasses before getting in her white Bentley and driving off.

"Desmond, please come in."

"Thank you for seeing me on such short notice, Angel," Desmond, said stepping inside the marble foyer of her home.

"You didn't leave me much of a choice. On the phone you made it sound like it was a do or die situation. I see you brought company with you too," Angel commented when Miles, Sammie, and Rico came in right behind Desmond.

"Yes, I forgot to mention that, but this is important. You know how much I value time and I wouldn't have tracked you down unless it was critical."

"What is so urgent that you had to see me immediately?"

"I know you're very close to Taren. I need you to show this gentleman," Desmond nodded his head acknowledging Rico, "a picture of her."

"Why? And what is this about?" Angel demanded to know.

"He might have some information pertaining to Laurie's death, but he needs to see a picture of Taren to be sure. Angel, can you please just show him the picture," he pleaded, noticing her resistance.

"Fine." Angel went and got her iPhone and pulled up some recent pictures she had taken with Taren and some of the other ladies that worked for Angel's Girls. "This is her."

"Yeah, that's the girl. Her hair wasn't blonde then, it was black, but she definitely the girl that was with Tony." Rico was adamant.

"Angel, I think Taren might be involved with Laurie's death," Desmond said.

"Because she knew Tony? Taren already told me she knew him months ago. She needed to make some extra money and started seeing him outside of work. She apologized, we dealt with it, and moved on," Angel stated matter-of-factly.

"Okay, but Clarissa told me..."

"Who the fuck is Clarissa?" she questioned cutting Desmond off.

"Clarissa was one of my dancers at the club. She was also best friends with Aspen," Desmond explained. "She told me that Aspen had some concerns about Taren's involvement in Laurie's death."

"That's the most absurd shit I've ever heard! Why in the hell would Taren kill Laurie? They were friends." Desmond could see Angel was agitated, but this was too important for him to back down from.

"I think because Laurie might've found out that Taren and Tony were working together and was responsible for the assault that landed her in the hospital."

"How dare you make those sorts of accusations against Taren. That's sick! When Laurie was in the hospital, Taren was right there by her side. You're unbelievable, Desmond." Angel was shaking her head ready to throw them all out her house.

"I get that you and Taren are extremely close."

"Yes, we are. I consider her to be family," Angel stressed.

"Point taken. But let's take the emotions out of it and look at the facts," Desmond pressed on. "There are too many things linking Taren with Tony."

"Are you not listening?! I already explained that to you," Angel scoffed.

"There's more. Aspen also told Clarissa that an earring Laurie was wearing on the night she got murdered, she saw it at Taren's place. Taren told Aspen that she had lied and Laurie did stop by her apartment after they all left the lounge and Laurie must've dropped the earring then."

"You must be mistaken," Angel said, putting her head down. She began thinking about every conversation she had with Taren regarding that night and if she ever mentioned seeing Laurie.

"No, Angel, I'm not mistaken. I have no reason to lie to you. We're business partners and we both want the same thing."

"There has to be a reasonable explanation and I know how to clear it up."

"How?"

"I'll get Taren on the phone. You can speak to her and you can ask her all the questions you like. She has nothing to hide," Angel said calling her best friend. "Wait, this can't be right."

"What's wrong?" Desmond asked walking closer to Angel. Sammie, Miles, and Rico were each looking at each other like this was the most uncomfortable shit ever.

"It's saying her phone is disconnected. Let me call her home phone." A few seconds later Angel hung up. "It's disconnected too."

"Can she not pay her bills... what's going on?" Desmond questioned. "When's the last time you spoke to her?"

"A few days ago. We had lunch. She said she was taking some time off to deal with a family emergency. I knew she would be leaving soon, but not this soon. I also don't understand why she disconnected her phones. It's not like she isn't coming back." Angel was baffled and didn't know what to think.

"Do you have any contact information for a family member she might be staying at?"

"Come to think of it I do. A few months ago, she went back home for about a week. She stayed at her aunt's house. I have the number in my phone," Angel said going to her contact list and making the call.

"Hello," a woman answered.

"Hi, is this Clara?"

"Yeah, who is this?"

"This is Angel. I'm good friends with your niece, Taren."

"Oh, I remember Taren talking about you. What

can I do for you... didn't nothing happen to my niece did it?"

"No, no. Umm, I was actually hoping she was staying there with you or you knew where she might be."

"Why would Taren be here? She living in Miami."

"Yes, but both her phones are disconnected and she told she was going home for a while to help take care of her mother," Angel told the woman.

"What in the hell are you talking about! My sister died four months ago of a drug overdose. What sort of sick game are you playing?"

"Taren's mom is dead?" Angel could barely get the question out.

"Yes, she's dead and if you were truly friends with my niece you would already know this. Now please don't call my house again," the woman yelled before hanging up the phone.

Angel stood frozen unable to move, she couldn't even speak. She felt a sharp pain like she was punched in the stomach and no air could get to her lungs.

"Angel, are you alright?" Desmond came over and put his arm around her. "Come sit down," he said taking her over to the sofa. "What did the woman tell you... Taren's not dead, is she?" Angel looked so distraught he could only imagine the worse.

"Not yet, but she's gonna be," Angel said, snapping out of her daze. "She played me."

"Talk to me."

"A few days ago, Taren and I met for lunch. She seemed stressed. After I wouldn't let up, she confided in me that her mother had taken a turn for the worse and was back on drugs. Her mother has been fighting addiction ever since Taren's father got killed a few years ago. Taren said she really wanted her mother to go to this rehab center, but it was super expensive. I volunteered to pay for it. I wrote her a check right there on the spot. Can't believe how stupid I am." Angel stared up at the ceiling. She was hurt and pissed off.

"You're not stupid. Taren knows you're a good person and she played on that. What did she do, take the money for her mom's rehab and run off?" Desmond asked.

"Her mother's dead. How sick can you be to lie on your mother like that? She died four months ago. When Taren went home around that time, it was probably for her mother's funeral. She didn't even tell me. I considered her to be my best friend, but I don't even know who she is. I have to find her. She can't get away with this."

"Do you have any idea where she might be?"

"None. I gave her enough money to go anywhere and start over. Where that might be, I have no idea,"

Angel said with disdain. "But I won't stop looking until I find Taren and bring her back to Miami." I will not rest until she's held responsible for Laurie's murder."

"Miss, would you care for another strawberry mimosa?" the waiter asked.

"Yes, I would. As a matter of fact, bring me two." Taren smiled, pulling down her Gigi Burris hat. Protecting her face from the hot Mexican sun. She was lounging by the pool at the five-star resort she was now calling home, at least for the moment.

Once Taren accepted there was no way she could get to Dominique and soon everyone would know all of her dirty deeds, she made the decision to bolt. It was rather easy. The only thing stopping her was money. When she realized Angel was still unaware of all her sins, there was a small window of using that to her advantage. That's when she conjured up the story about wanting to send her already deceased mother to rehab. Right after their lunch date, Taren wasted no time going to the bank and cashing the check. She would've caught a flight that day but her bank put a temporary hold due to the high amount. But the moment it cleared, Taren cashed out and left Miami in the dust.

Now here she was starting over in Mexico. She cut off her phone and got a new number and carrier, wanting to erase all traces of her past life. Taren even had a new identity. She no longer had to worry, but that didn't keep her from thinking about what she considered unfinished business back in Miami. Taren no longer had her mother or father and she blamed Angel for both of their deaths. In her mind, if her father had never gotten killed then her mother would've never turned to drugs to cope.

So, for now, Taren would keep a very low profile. She would enjoy her time relaxing by the pool, lounging at the beach and indulging in alcoholic drinks. When the time was right, she would sneak back to Miami and make Angel pay for all the misery she had caused her.

Chapter Sixteen

Craving You

"I'm loving this hotel room." Aaliyah gasped when she came into her mother's top floor, one-bedroom suite. "This looks like Egyptian marble."

"I'm sure you would know better than me," Precious remarked. "I just like things to look luxurious. I don't know all the details. Clearly you get that trait from Supreme. He can give you the specifics of anything high end."

"And you're perched atop the city," Aaliyah said,

moving back the lush curtains. "These floor-to-ceiling windows give you endless views of Biscayne Bay, Key Biscayne, and South Beach. I'm jealous. Maybe Dale and I can stay here for our honeymoon."

"Aren't you all going to some exotic island for your honeymoon."

"Yes, who said we can't have two honeymoons. One someplace else and the other when we get back to Miami," Aaliyah said casually. "With everything we've been through lately we deserve it, especially Dale."

"How is he? When I came over the other day he seemed like he was doing really good. Is he still improving?"

"Yes! I can't believe how smoothly his recovery is going. Yesterday we went to the doctor for a checkup and he was even impressed."

"Baby, I'm so happy to hear that. The fear and pain I saw in your eyes during this ordeal, I don't ever want to see you like that again. It really broke my heart," Precious revealed. "It brought back all those memories of when I thought Supreme was dead. At that time, the only reason I wanted to live was to get revenge against the person who I thought was responsible for his death. It was such a dark period in my life."

"I love when you open up to me like this. The older I get the more I appreciate it. I have a deeper understanding now that I'm with the man I want to spend the rest of my life with."

"If you have a deeper understanding now, wait until you have kids of your own. That's a different type of love and it cuts much deeper if something goes wrong. I'm always worrying about you and Xavier. It doesn't matter how old you get or how independent you are."

"I got a glimpse of that when Dad thought Angel had died in the explosion. I've never seen him look so devastated." Sadness crept across Aaliyah's face. "I don't think he forgives me for leaving the club without her."

"Aaliyah, Nico understands that was a stressful situation for everyone. He doesn't blame you. Angel chose to stay in the club. You wanted her to get out too."

"I did, but her decision makes me look so bad in our father's eyes."

"What are you talking about?" Precious stood up from the chair in the sitting room and went over to sit down next to her daughter.

"Angel was more concerned about saving someone else's life than her own. How selfless is that. I would never." Aaliyah sighed. "I mean, if it was you, Xavier, one of my dads, Dale, then of course, but a stranger... definitely not," she admitted.

"Because you're being honest and you feel that

way, you think that makes you look bad to your dad?"

"All I'm saying is that I'm already known for being spoiled and feeling entitled, but so is Justina and even Amir, so I never have a reason to feel guilty about it. Now here comes Angel. No mother, lost her grandmother, grew up with no money, no daddy, having to take care of herself, but instead of her being angry with the world she's generous and forgiving. I mean, I wasn't exactly welcoming her as my sister, yet she went out her way to get me and Justina out of that bathroom. When Daddy looks at her, I can tell he's proud to call her his daughter."

"He's proud of you too, Aaliyah. Nico adores you. You know that," Precious said, lifting her daughter's face up.

"It's not the same. Then he feels all this guilt for not being in her life while she was growing up. Even though it's not his fault. He didn't know about her."

"I do agree with you that Nico feels guilty. But I think it has more to do with his relationship with Angel's mother," Precious rationalized. "He feels like he let Lisa down and because of that his daughter grew up without her father. This is new for Nico just like it is for you. But he loves you and he has always been proud to call you his daughter," she stated adamantly. "I don't know Angel very well, but she does seem like a wonderful young woman. Given what she's been through, I'm sure Nico is extremely proud of her, but that doesn't diminish his feelings for you."

"Maybe you're right. I guess I see so much of Daddy in Angel and I know he does too. Because of that, she might be his favorite."

"Aaliyah, this isn't a competition. She's your sister. Maybe you should put more energy into getting to know Angel instead of worrying she's going to take your place in Nico's heart. That will never happen. Nico has enough love for both of you."

"Thank you for telling me that." Aaliyah reached over and hugged her mother. "I know I don't say it enough, but you really are the best mom ever."

"And you're the best daughter. I'm glad you were able to stop by before I go back to New York tomorrow."

"Me too. I wish we could've spent more time together, but circumstances didn't allow that. But having you here has been great. Your support helped me more than you know."

"Aaliyah, if you need me to come back before the wedding, all you have to do is ask and I'm on the next plane. I'm your mother and I'll always have your back."

Precious and Aaliyah spent the next couple hours laughing, exchanging stories, and imagining how Aaliyah's life will be as a married woman.

Justina had just gotten out the shower when she heard the doorbell. *Who could that be,* she thought not expecting anyone to stop by. Knowing that Nesa wasn't dead yet, Justina decided not to take any chances and retrieved her gun from the drawer by her bed. She turned down the piano music playing in the background and walked quietly to the door. Justina looked out the peephole and her cautious demeanor changed.

"Just a minute!" she called out, putting her gun away before opening the door. "You are the last person I expected to see."

"The back and forth missed phone calls was becoming pointless. Did I catch you at a bad time?" Desmond asked, seeing Justina in a silk bathrobe with wet hair.

"I was in the shower, but I'm done now. Come sit down. Can I get you something to drink?"

"No. I'm not staying long. I wanted to see you in person. Make sure you were doing okay."

"I appreciate you checking up on me. I did try calling you back a couple times, but like you said, we kept missing each other."

Justina sat down on the couch and crossed

her legs. Given her attire it wouldn't take much to look sexy, but she didn't want Desmond to think she was trying to seduce him even though she was. His sudden visit couldn't have come at a more ideal time for her.

"Is your boyfriend still in town?"

"If you thought he was, do you think it's appropriate for you to show up here unannounced?"

"There's nothing going on between us other than we've done some business together and I consider you to be an acquaintance who I care about."

"True. And to answer your question my boyfriend went back to New York. He won't be back until Aaliyah and Dale's wedding."

"I see. Maybe you'll have a chance to introduce me to him at the wedding."

"If you like, but I'm sure you didn't come over here to talk about my boyfriend." Justina tilted her head to the side and swept her hair over her shoulder. The longer she stared at him the more she envisioned him in her bed.

Desmond was casually dressed in a lightweight, blue fog-colored, trim fit, short sleeve, Peruvian cotton V-neck t-shirt and relaxed fit jogger pants. But it wasn't the clothes he had on that was turning Justina on, it was his solid cut six foot-two frame. There didn't appear to be an ounce of fat on his body, but as busy as he was running his multiple businesses, she couldn't fathom how he would have the time to do the workout needed to maintain such a sculpted frame.

"Besides checking on you, I also wanted to personally invite you to the grand reopening of my club," Desmond said, handing Justina an invite.

"This is very elegant," she said observing the royal gold on white pearl invite. "You move fast. Very impressive."

"Thank you. Does that mean you'll be there?"

"Only if you want me to."

"I wouldn't have come if I didn't."

"Then I'll be there. I'm not trying to get rid of you, but I really need to get dressed. There's somewhere I have to be. I'll show you out." Justina stood up and allowed her bathrobe to slightly open revealing her naked body. She did it so smoothly, it appeared to be a genuine accident.

"Oh gosh, I'm so embarrassed." Justina put her head down and quickly tied her bathrobe back up, but she had accomplished what she set out to do. Her freshly bathed, glistening skin had Desmond open. He was already physically attracted to her, this just took it to the next level.

"You have absolutely nothing to be embarrassed about," Desmond said as he locked eyes with Justina with such intensity, they had to be imagining doing the exact same thing to each other. "I better be going." Desmond finally broke their stare.

"What if I don't want you to go?" Justina realized if she didn't speak up now and make it clear she wanted him, Desmond would walk out the door no matter how tempted he might be.

"I think you do," he said heading towards the door.

Justina followed behind him and put her hand on his arm. "No, I want you to stay."

"If I stay, you know what that means don't you?"

"I do."

Right after Justina said those words, Desmond was grasping the back of her hair and his tongue was down her throat. Their kiss was passionate and intense as their lust for each other. She led him to her bed, taking his clothes off along the way. His body was even more delectable than Justina envisioned it to be. She wanted to devour every inch of him like he was the perfect dessert. No words were exchanged between the two, except the sounds of heightened pleasure.

For the next couple of hours, Desmond and Justina gave into their desires for each other. She'd been longing to have every inch of his thickness inside her and he craved to feel her wetness. Now that their bodies had become one, it was only a matter of time before their minds and souls did too.

Chapter Seventeen

I See You

Dirk was about to give up on tracking down Nesa. If he wasn't so desperate for a hefty payday, he would've gave this hit deuces after being doused with pepper spray. But his persistence was finally paying off. After sleeping in his car for the past two days, parked near Nesa's apartment, there had been zero activity until now. Around two o'clock in the morning, Dirk noticed a man go into Nesa's apartment. He went in with nothing, but came out with a tote bag after staying less than fifteen minutes. When Dirk recognized the car he was driving being the same one Nesa was in when he hit her, he knew he might be on to something.

Dirk followed the man to a hotel and he was positive this was where Nesa had been staying. Now he needed to figure out which room and the only person who could help him with that was the man in the car. Dirk ran up on him so fast, he didn't even see him coming.

"I want yo' room key and room number or I'ma blow yo' fuckin' head off," Dirk warned pressing his Desert Eagle .50 caliber against the back of the man's head.

"Man, I ain't got nothing in my room. I got like forty dollars in my wallet and you can have it."

"Nigga, you can keep yo' forty dollars. I don't want that shit. I told you what I want, now give it up," Dirk demanded.

"I don't have no room key."

"Then what's yo' room number?"

"I don't remember," he stuttered. "I'm visiting somebody."

"What's her name?"

"It's a guy. His name is Malcom."

"Call Malcom right now and ask him for the room number. Don't do nothing stupid or I'll kill you."

"My phone is in my back pocket."

"Get it out!"

His fingers were shaking while dialing the number.

"TJ, what's taking you so long?!" Nesa asked when she answered.

"We on the way up, but I forgot the room number."

"We! Who tha fuck you got wit you?! Don't be bringing no motherfuckers up in here."

"Malcom, you gon' give me the room number or what?"

"He hung up on me," TJ said shrugging.

"Nigga, you think I'm stupid! That was a female who answered the phone and I bet it was that chick Nesa since you driving her car. Now give me that damn room number."

"I told you I don't know it."

"You ready to die for that bitch!"

"She my cousin! I ain't gon' let you run up in there and kill her. Please, let me go. I don't have nothing to do with this."

"Then give me the room number."

"Like I said, I don't know it." That was TJ's story and he was sticking to it. He figured if he didn't give Dirk the room number, the gunman would say fuck it, let him go and try to figure out another way to get to Nesa. Unfortunately, TJ had no idea how desperate Dirk was and desperation led to reckless decisions.

"Man, fuck it. I gave you a chance,' Dirk huffed, releasing one bullet and blowing TJ's brains out. His body slumped to the ground dying instantly.

"Oh fuck! That nigga must've found me!" Nesa was freaking out as she gathered her stuff to leave.

TJ said 'We are on our way up,' that means the guy had to be downstairs. He was warning me, that's why he called me Malcom. The guy is probably outside or in the lobby. But where is TJ? He has the key to my car. Fuck, let me call an Uber to pick me up, but it can't be from here. I'll take the stairs and go out the back and have the car pick me up across the street. Yeah, that's what I'll do, Nesa decided as she now felt like a woman on the run.

"What time are your sister and Justina coming over?" Dale asked Aaliyah while brushing his hair in the bathroom.

Aaliyah glanced down at her watch, "In about

twenty or thirty minutes. Where are you off to?"

"I have to meet up with Desmond and discuss some business."

"I know you're loving being behind the wheel of the car all by yourself," she said, walking up behind Dale and wrapping her arms around his bare chest. "Don't we look good together." Aaliyah smiled, looking at their reflection in the mirror.

"Yes, it feels great driving my own cars again and yes we do look good together."

"Can you believe in a few short weeks we'll be married?"

"I can believe it. I can't wait to call you my wife."

"And you'll be my husband," she whispered in his ear, then kissed Dale on his neck. "I feel like the luckiest woman in the world."

"And I'm the luckiest man."

"Can I be honest with you about something." Aaliyah said.

"Yes. I want you to always be honest with me."

"When you first came out your coma, I was worried. Especially because of the gaps in your memory."

"Yeah, it concerned me too. I still don't remember everything, but my mind doesn't feel scrambled like it did the first couple of weeks after I woke up."

"I know you don't have any memory from the night of the explosion, but has it been hard on you remembering that Emory is no longer here?"

"At first. You know how close I was to my brother. Even with all his fucked up ways, he was my brother and I loved him. He was supposed to be standing by my side, being the best man at my wedding. That's not gonna happen and I have to accept it. But you know what's the hardest thing for me?"

"What?"

"Being no closer to finding out who killed him. The police say they haven't closed the case and the investigation into his murder is still ongoing, but that's some bullshit. They've thrown his file in the corner with all the rest. I had my own people investigating, but the streets ain't talking. I feel like I'll never get justice for my brother. That shit is gon' eat away at me for the rest of my life," Dale declared.

"Baby, in time it'll get better. Emory knew how much you loved him. He wouldn't want you to spend all your time and energy looking for his killer. He would want you to live your life and be happy."

"Maybe you're right. Maybe that is what my brother would want for me. I guess if it's meant for me to know the truth about why he died and who killed him, I won't have to search, the information will come to me. What do you think?" Dale questioned.

"I think what you said is absolutely correct." Aaliyah leaned in and kissed Dale. "The most important thing is we have each other. Nothing else matters," Aaliyah then gave Dale another kiss, this one much longer until they were interrupted. "That's the doorbell. One of the ladies must be here. I wonder who made it first." She smiled excitedly.

"Aren't you enthusiastic." Dale smirked.

"Baby, we're discussing our wedding, so of course I'm enthusiastic!" She nuzzled the tip of her nose against Dale's. "I love you, babe."

"I love you more." They blew each other kisses before Aaliyah disappeared to go downstairs to open the door.

"Surprise!" Angel and Justina said simultaneously when Aaliyah opened the door.

"This I wasn't expecting! Both of you are here at the exact same time. I'm impressed!" Aaliyah beamed. "Come in, ladies."

"I was shocked when I pulled up and Angel was getting out her car. I guess we were both looking forward to coming," Justina said as they followed Aaliyah outside to the courtyard. They sat down on the loggia lined expansive terrace that overlooked the garden and secluded pool area.

"This is really nice, Aaliyah. Champagne, hors d'oeuvres, dessert. Very classy. I feel special," Angel commented.

"I did have it catered. I wanted both of my maid of honors to know how much I appreciate them."

"I'm sorry, did I miss something... you said both?" Justina questioned. "I thought I was your maid of honor?"

"You are, but I decided to have two. That is if Angel accepts." Aaliyah turned to Angel and smiled.

"Yes! It would mean the world to me. I'm stunned."

"So am I." Justina mumbled under her breath, taking a sip of champagne.

"I hope our father didn't make you do this. If so, it really isn't necessary," Angel wanted Aaliyah to know.

"Our dad had nothing to do with this. This is all me and what I want. After the explosion and almost losing Dale, it made me put a lot of things in perspective. We're family, Angel, and I really want to get to know you. I hope this gesture shows you how sincere I am about doing that."

"It does. Growing up, not knowing who my father was and my mother being dead, having a sister didn't even seem like a possibility. Now within less than a year, I have a father and a sister. Aaliyah, I wasn't sure if you would ever embrace me as a member of your family, but now that you have, thank you." Angel stood up so she could give Aaliyah a hug.

Justina was on her second glass of champagne trying to drink away the repulsion she felt watching the lovefest between Aaliyah and Angel. *Gosh, can they be any more disgusting. I mean really, Aaliyah wouldn't know how to be sincere about anything, even if it slapped her in the face. And poor Angel is so desperate to belong, she'll believe whatever bullshit her so-called sister shoves down her throat. This sisterly union won't last long once Angel realizes that Aaliyah is only happy when the world is revolving around her self-centered ass,* Justina was ready to burst out laughing at the thought.

"Justina, I hope you don't mind sharing the maid of honor duties with me," Angel said.

"Do I mind... what kind of question is that? You saved my life. Honestly, I don't even feel worthy to share the duties with you."

"Justina, don't say that. Not only are you worthy, but you're my best friend. She's being very modest right now." Aaliyah glanced over at Angel before continuing. "But Justina actually saved my life... literally. I was about to be shot by a deranged woman named Maya. She was really my aunt, but I refuse to claim her. So yeah, she was about to kill me and my mother. Luckily, Justina showed up when she did or I wouldn't be sitting here able to tell you this story."

Angel's mouth was left wide open listening to what Aaliyah divulged. "I wasn't ready for all that." Angel shook her head. "You really are a best friend."

"Yes she is... but you all excuse me for one

second. I need to go speak to Dale before he leaves," Aaliyah said excusing herself from the table.

"This Maya woman, is she related to Aaliyah on her mother or father's side?" Angel asked Justina.

"Her mother. Maya is, I mean, she was Precious's sister."

"So, Maya is dead?"

"Yes, I killed her. I didn't have a choice. I needed to protect Aaliyah."

"This Maya woman sounds disturbed."

'That's one way of describing her. Maya put her family through hell. That drama dates way back. We would need more than one bottle of champagne to peel back all the layers of that saga," Justina scoffed.

"Let me know when you're up to it. I would love to hear that story from beginning to end," Angel said, biting down on a cocktail shrimp.

"We can have a girl's slumber party and I can give you all the deets then," Justina joked.

"Sounds like fun!"

"I'm sure it would be, but listen, I briefly touched on it earlier, now I want to elaborate. What you did for Aaliyah and me that night was commendable. You risked your life for us and I'll forever be grateful to you, so thank you."

"You're welcome, but I really wish everyone would stop making such a big deal about what I did. Under the circumstances I believe mostly anybody would've done the same. Even the other woman I went back for. What's her name?" Angel was having trouble remembering.

"I don't know that woman or her name," Justina hurried up and said.

"Really? That's so strange. When I went to get her, she mentioned you."

"Are you sure? What did she say?"

"Not much. She was a little out of it, but she kept saying where's Justina." I thought for sure you all knew each other."

"No. I had seen her before a couple times when I stopped by the club. That's why I went over to see if she was still alive because her face seemed familiar," Justina explained. "I didn't think she was alive though."

"Yeah, you mentioned to us you thought she was dead."

"I did. I was shocked when I saw you coming out the club carrying her."

"She was really out of it when I went back for her, but I could definitely tell she was alive."

"When I saw her, she didn't look like she was breathing. Her eyes were closed and she appeared to be lifeless. But it was so dark in there and I was scared, ready to get out so I completely misjudged. Thank goodness you went back... oh here comes Aaliyah!" Justina quickly said, doing her best to end any further discussion about Nesa. She wanted that woman erased from her memory permanently.

"Dale told me to tell you ladies hello," Aaliyah said sitting back down.

"Why didn't he come out and tell us that himself?" Justina asked.

"He wanted to, but he was running late for his business meeting with Desmond."

"I had no idea Desmond was doing business with Dale," Angel remarked.

"Why would you?" Justina questioned, sounding a tad territorial.

"Angel and Desmond are business partners." Aaliyah volunteered the information before Angel had a chance to answer.

"Wow, very interesting."

"What's so interesting about that?" Angel gave Justina a wicked glare.

"I didn't know that Desmond's partner was a female."

"We're only partners in Angel's Girls. I'm not a part of his other business ventures."

"Oh." Justina's one word response did nothing to help her cause. It only heightened Angel's suspicion.

"For a second I thought you were jealous because you seem to be very protective of Desmond. Is he your man because last I heard he was single."

Aaliyah almost spit out her champagne when

Angel made her bold comments. She quickly went into damage control before Justina had a chance to clap back.

"Justina is Amir's girlfriend. They are very much in love. He was here recently to check up on her after the explosion. He had to go back to New York, but he'll be here for the wedding. I can't wait for you to meet him," Aaliyah added.

Aaliyah's attempt to put out the fire didn't work. The frown Justina was famous for getting when pissed off, was still plastered on her face.

"That's right, I forgot you were in a relationship, Justina. I guess it's crazy of me to think you would be jealous of my relationship with Desmond when your man is Amir," Angel mocked.

"No worries." Justina smiled sweetly. "Now that I think about it, I did sound a bit possessive," she said laughing. "I do consider Desmond to be a friend, but of course that doesn't mean he's obligated to tell me every facet of his life."

"Men never do. They're notorious for keeping secrets," Aaliyah quipped.

"So true. I can only imagine all the secrets Darien has kept from me," Angel joked, carrying on like she hadn't just come for Justina's throat on the sly.

"Enough about our men, let's talk about my wedding!" Aaliyah gushed. Angel and Justina played along, smiling like they were all the best of friends.

Let me find out you a slick bitch, Justina thought to herself, cutting her eyes at Angel. *I caught the shade and I know you were trying to get a rise out of me, but I didn't take the bait although I was tempted. I have to be careful how I play you because you ain't no dummy. That's the only reason I chose to let that shit you said about Desmond slide. You thought I was going to snap back and so did Aaliyah, but that would've only made you feel justified to be all up in my shit. But by me playing it cool, you had no choice but calm down and let it go or you risked coming across as petty. I see you Mrs. Angel Blaze.*

Chapter Eighteen

Scandalous

"She's waking up," the nurse told Miles who was in Dominique's hospital room.

"I'll go let Desmond know."

"Please apologize to Mr. Blackwell for me again. When I called you before she was fully awake, but then she fell back asleep before you arrived. I know he's a busy man and I don't want him to think I was wasting his time," the nurse explained.

"It's fine. I told Desmond and he understands

the medicine Dominique's on has her sleeping a lot. Let me go get him before she falls asleep again."

Miles rushed out to go locate his boss. Desmond was understanding, but he also was an impatient man. If it wasn't for the fact that he had a soft spot for Dominique, he probably would've gotten rid of her nurse a long time ago.

"There you are," Miles said walking up on Desmond who was on the phone.

"Justina, let me call you back... what is it, Miles?" he questioned, easily transitioning from one conversation to another.

"Dominique is awake."

"Awake, awake?" Desmond wanted to confirm.

"Yes." Miles nodded.

"Cool."

When the two men got to Dominique's room she was sitting up drinking water. "Desmond!" her eyes lit up with joy.

"I haven't seen you smile like that since you've been here," the nurse remarked, startled at how happy her patient seemed.

"Are you the one who got me all these flowers?" Dominque asked.

"You know it. I had to make sure my number one girl was surrounded by beauty. Beautiful flowers for a beautiful girl."

"I don't feel beautiful." Dominique put her head

down as if embarrassed by her appearance."

"You're just as beautiful if not more than the day I met you at that club." Desmond gave her a re-assuring smile. "Now if you all will excuse us, I need to speak to Dominique privately. I need everyone to leave... now."

The two men hired to guard Dominique, Miles and Sammie, all began to exit quickly, but the nurse lingered behind.

"When I said everyone leave that includes you," Desmond looked at the nurse and said.

"I'm so sorry. If Dominique needs anything, I'll be right outside in the hallway.

"I can't tell you how happy I am to see you," Dominique beamed when Desmond sat down next to her.

"I'm happy to see you too."

"You're not mad at me?"

"Why would I be mad at you?" Desmond was puzzled by her question.

"If it wasn't for me, your club would've never been demolished in that explosion."

"You didn't set off that bomb."

"I know, but I brought the person to your club. I swear I didn't know she had a bomb. She promised to let me go if I didn't tell the police or anyone else what she did. I was supposed to tell them I had been kidnapped, but I never saw the person's face." Dominique's eyes began to water up as she remembered everything that happened that night. "I can't believe all those people died because of me," she cried.

"Dominique, stop!" Desmond leaned over and pulled her close in his arms. "You were a victim. I'm just glad you survived.

"Oh gosh! She killed Clarissa's friend too!" she blurted out as if that memory had just popped in her head.

"You're talking about Aspen?" Desmond asked letting Dominique go.

"Yes! That's her name. Clarissa asked me to stop by and drop off her driver's license. I had to use the bathroom and while I was in there I heard a gun go off. I was so scared that I stayed in the bathroom. Then she came back later on that night and found me. She held me hostage at her apartment until the night of the explosion. Those were the darkest days of my life," Dominique sobbed.

"You're safe now." Desmond wiped away her tears. She looked like a lost, helpless, scared little girl with her bare face, loose bun, and rosy cheeks. He wanted to save her. "Who did this to you, Dominique?"

"I don't know her last name, but I remember when I was in the bathroom and I heard the women arguing, Aspen called her Taren. Taren is the one who almost ruined my life," Dominique wept.

Desmond held Dominque closely doing his best to contain the rage that was simmering inside him, ready to explode. He was having a difficult time wrapping his mind around the notion that one woman was responsible for all this bloodshed. Laurie's murder was one thing, but taking down his club, killing Aspen and all the people who died from the explosion... but why is what he wanted to know. In the larger scheme of things, the reason didn't matter to Desmond. Taren had to go and if he had to turn the world upside down to find her, then he would.

"Any news about Taren?" Angel questioned the private investigator. She was using the same man that found her father, so she was hoping he would have the same luck tracking down Taren.

"The last location I have on her is Texas," he said.

"Texas? Why in the hell would Taren be in Texas," Angel wondered.

"Does she have family there or old boyfriends?"

"Not that I know of. Besides her aunt, the only other relative she ever mentioned was an uncle who lived in Chicago."

"She might've just stopped through here. I'm going to head to Texas and see if I can find out anything. I'll go to Chicago too. But don't worry, I'll find her dead or alive."

"Preferably alive. We have some unfinished business."

"I'm on it. I'll call you with an update as soon as I have one," he said before ending their call.

Angel put her phone down and became lost in trying to deal with her emotions, standing on the bedroom terrace overlooking the reflecting pool that had a glass mosaic floor. The sparkling jewel, set against lusciously landscaped greenery, was always a calming escape for Angel. It was like a little piece of heaven right there within her grasp. But even with all that peaceful exquisiteness in her view, it did nothing to help her escape the fury she felt towards Taren. She wanted to believe that the woman she had considered to be like a sister to her had a valid excuse for killing Laurie and even lying about her mother, but Angel couldn't come up with one. That infuriated her even more.

"What you out here thinking about?" Darien's voice shook Angel out of her thoughts.

"I'm not thinking, just enjoying the view."

"Save it. You always come out here and stand in that exact location when you have a lot on your mind."

"You know me too well."

"You are my wife. That should be mandatory. Let me guess, you're thinking about Taren."

Angel turned away for a moment before responding to what Darien said. "How can you think you know someone so well, but then find out you don't know them at all. Taren has been a part of my life since I was a little girl. I know she's capable of murder, anyone is under certain circumstances. But I would never in a million years believe she was capable of killing Laurie or lying to me about it. Or telling me her dead mother needs to go to rehab so she could take my money and start a new life somewhere else. This is not the best friend I grew up with."

"Maybe you didn't know Taren as well as you thought."

"That's an understatement. I'm beginning to think I don't know her at all. It makes me wonder what else Taren's capable of."

"Probably just about anything," Darien figured. "Right now everything is fresh so you're caught up in your feelings, but this too shall pass, so try not to worry so much, babe," he said giving Angel a sweet kiss on her forehead.

"Thank you for your words of encouragement and listening to me. I know you're sick of me discussing Taren every single day because I'm sick of talking about her. I'ma do better. I feel like I'm obsessed with confronting her with everything I know, but need to sit back and let things play out. I'm going back to work next week and start focusing on Angel's Girls. That will keep me busy and my mind off Taren."

"You can also go with me to Vegas while I train for this upcoming fight."

"Gosh, baby, how could I forget about that? I've had so much on my mind that's coming up. When are you leaving to start training?"

"Friday," Darien reminded her.

"So soon? Wow, how long will you be there?"

"For the next two or three months."

"I promise I'll come join you as soon as things are situated here. I want to get Angel's Girls back running properly. Desmond has been so focused on reopening Diamonds & Pearls that our business has taken a backseat. The ladies are maintaining, but the money isn't coming in nearly the way it should."

"You know how I feel about the company. I wish you would let it go. It's not like you need the money."

"You have boxing and I have Angel's Girls. Let's just leave it at that." Darien knew that was his wife's way of saying conversation over.

"Point made," Darien said, slipping his fingers in between Angel's. "All I want is for you to be happy."

"I am happy. Even with this Taren drama, life

is good. I have the most amazing husband, a great father, and Aaliyah is finally embracing me as her sister. Did I mention how amazing my husband is?" She giggled, kissing Darien. "I wish we could stand here looking into each other's eyes all day, but I have to go meet Desmond."

"Is everything okay?"

"Yeah, he said he wanted to talk to me about Dominique."

"Isn't that the woman from the club you've been looking for?"

"Yes."

"Did Desmond find her?" Darien questioned.

"He said he didn't want to elaborate over the phone, but it must be important. He was adamant I met with him today."

"Don't let me hold you up. Go handle your business. I'll see you later on tonight for dinner."

"I didn't know we had dinner plans." Angel smiled. "Are we taking me someplace romantic?"

"Yes. Every day until I have to leave for training, we gon' do something romantic. I'ma spoil you to the point, you'll be rushing to be with me in Vegas, 'cause you miss me so fuckin' much."

"I'm missing you already." Angel sprinkled seductive kisses on Darien's neck.

"Don't start something you can't finish," he said becoming aroused.

"Desmond can wait, but our bed can't," Angel teased. "While you're spoiling me, I'ma spoil you too. Come on," she said leading him into their bedroom. "Let's go make love."

"Mmmm, don't stop, baby. You feel so good," Justina moaned as Desmond went deeper and deeper with each stroke. "I love this dick," she purred, breathing heavily in his ear while taking the tips of her fingers and rubbing the nipples on his chest. Justina knew it drove him crazy and made Desmond cum even harder.

Since the first time having sex a few weeks ago, they had been at it nonstop. They were like two dogs in heat. Justina used her overactive sex drive to lure Desmond out of his comfort zone. In the past, sex was simply a form of stress release for him. His focus was work and making money. Sex was an afterthought because it was always readily available. But Justina made sex different for Desmond. It was no longer an afterthought, it became a priority. So, when Justina showed up at his office unexpectedly, got down on her knees, wrapped her moist lips around his hardened dick, and began to deep throat him, he couldn't resist. Now they were on his desk with Justina's legs draped around his waist and him thrusting in and out.

"We gotta stop doing this," Desmond said putting his pants back on.

"Doing what? I didn't know we were doing anything wrong." Justina smiled, buttoning up her blouse. "Are you coming over tonight?"

"Do you want me to?" He gave Justina this look that caught her off guard.

"I wouldn't have asked the question if I didn't. Or maybe you're giving me that look because you already have other plans and you have no intentions of coming."

"Other plans like what, Justina?"

"To go see that chick you put up in that high-rise apartment."

"I told you Dominique is a friend and she's also a dancer at my club. I'm helping her out, that's all."

"Do you help out all your dancers like that?" Justina shot back. "No need to answer. I don't even care," she said shrugging. "Don't come tonight. I can find something or someone else to do tonight," she said staring in her handheld mirror, applying some lipstick.

"What did you say to me?" Desmond stopped what he was doing, putting down the memo he was reading.

"Which part... that you didn't have to come

over or I would find something or someone else to do tonight." Justina repeated while continuing to touch up her makeup, but not making any eye contact with Desmond.

When Desmond reached over and held Justina's hair firmly in his grasp and said, "Do you really wanna play that game with me?" Justina was stunned. She was rarely speechless, but she wasn't expecting to get that reaction from Desmond. "Answer me." He gripped her hair even tighter. "You think I'ma stand here and let you disrespect me by saying you gonna fuck another nigga tonight."

"You already know I have a man. Don't you think I fuck him?" Justina taunted.

"You haven't fucked him since I've been inside of you," Desmond stated.

"It's only a matter of time. He'll be back soon."

Desmond released Justina from his grasp before he did something he regretted, like punch her in the mouth.

"I'm sorry." She walked up from behind and whispered in Desmond's ear. "I shouldn't have said that. I just hate knowing someone else has your attention other than me."

"Is that what you want, Justina... to have my full attention?"

"Yes! I don't like to share. I've never been good at that."

"I've never been good at sharing either. That's why you can't say dumb shit like that to me. I don't respond well."

"I don't respond well to you taking care of another woman," Justina seethed.

"Dominique is a friend and I don't cut off my friends."

"Fine," Justina hissed, grabbing her purse.

"Where are you going?" Desmond clutched her arm. He stared into Justina's eyes and there was this intriguing mystique he was drawn to although he knew he should let her go, but he couldn't. He wanted her and she wanted him too, but neither cared to admit just how much.

"I'm going to the spa to be pampered and get a massage, so I can be relaxed when you come over tonight. Because I know you're coming."

Desmond was still gripping Justina's arm, but he didn't let go, instead he pulled her close to his chest as he stared down at her. She looked up, seducing him with her eyes. They were ready to have sex again right there on his desk.

"I'll be there."

"Of course you will, and I'll be waiting for you." Their lips once again met and instantly the kisses went from soft to intense until Desmond's assistant knocked at the door.

"Mr. Blackwell, Angel is here to see you."

"Fuck!" Justina mumbled.

"Tell her I'll be out shortly," Desmond called out.

"Another one of your women coming to see you," Justina scoffed.

"Stop it. I already explained my relationship with Angel to you and she's a happily married woman."

"I know, but I want you all to myself," she admitted.

"Don't say it unless you mean it," Desmond cautioned.

"I do."

"It won't happen until you end that other situation you're in for good."

"I know, but I need some time."

"I'm not a patient man, Justina. Either you want me all to yourself or you wanna share me. You decide."

"I better go, but let me leave out first. I don't need Angel playing detective," Justina told him.

"Okay, I'll see you tonight."

When Justina walked out Desmond's office, Angel was sitting on the couch with her legs crossed, wearing a pair of pink/blue multi Choca Criss Louboutin that she had been eyeing, but hadn't gotten around to buying just yet. Seeing as though they had the same taste in shoes, Justina was glad Angel was a happily married woman because more than likely they would have the same taste in men. When she told Desmond she wanted his full attention, Justina meant it.

"I thought that was your white Bentley parked out front," Angel remarked standing up.

"You thought right. I absolutely love those shoes you're wearing."

"Thanks and I love your blouse. But I think you forgot to finish buttoning it up, unless you're going for that show your bra look. By the way, how is Desmond?"

"Good. He's looking forward to seeing you. I better be going. I have a lot of things I need to get done. It was great seeing you." Justina smiled demurely.

"Great seeing you too." Angel waved.

So, you are fucking Desmond, she thought, shaking her head. *I knew it and now my suspicions have been confirmed. You're scandalous, Justina. I wonder what your man Amir would think of your illicit sexcapades, or better yet Aaliyah,* Angel thought to herself entering Desmond's office. There was something about Justina she didn't trust. Now that she knew her business partner and her sister's best friend were fucking on the low, Angel was determined to get all the details on how long this sordid relationship had been going on.

Chapter Nineteen

Dead Weight

"Angel, have a seat," Desmond said closing his office door. "Can I get you anything?"

"No, I'm good. I saw Justina leaving. I didn't realize the two of you are so close," Angel remarked, sitting down in a chair facing Desmond's desk.

"I'm consulting her on a potential business investment," he said casually, like he didn't just have her bent over his desk.

"I'm sure she appreciates your business expertise."

"She does, but I didn't ask you here to discuss Justina. I have news regarding Dominique," Desmond stated.

"Is she dead?" Angel was nervous as she waited to hear Desmond's response.

"No, she's alive and doing much better."

"Thank goodness!" Relief swept through Angel. Where is she staying? I want to see her."

"I'll set something up soon."

"Set something up... what does that mean?" Angel was perplexed with his word usage.

"Dominique is living at one of my apartments for the time being," Desmond revealed.

"You said she was a dancer at your club, but I didn't know you all had the sort of relationship where you would have her living at one of your apartments."

"It's important to me that Dominique has everything she needs. What she went through was extremely traumatic. Having my people care for her guarantees she's straight."

"Have you let my father know you've found Dominique?"

"I did speak to Nico earlier to let him know Dominique was under my protection."

"Why do I have the feeling that even though

you're telling my father and I about Dominique today, you've known where she is for much longer."

"Listen, my club was under attack," Desmond said, sitting on the edge of his desk staring at Angel. "Nico took things personally because of you and Aaliyah. I took it personally because everyone in that club was my responsibility. All those people who died in my club, that shit will forever fuck wit' me. So, I didn't want anyone, including your father speaking to Dominique until I did."

"Okay, you spoke to her... now what?"

"Taren is the one responsible for detonating that bomb in my club and from here on out, I will be the one to deal with her."

"Are you sure it was Taren? I saw the video, it didn't look like her."

"It was. The footage only showed the woman from the back. With a wig and a hat, it could've been almost anybody but it wasn't. Dominique confirmed it was Taren."

Angel turned away, putting her head down. Her stomach became nauseated and she thought she was going to be sick. "Taren did this, but why?"

"I was hoping you could answer that question."

"I can't. Never did I think she was capable of anything like this. I was having a hard time believing she killed Laurie. Now you're telling me she blew up your club?" Angel shook her head in disbelief.

"She also killed Aspen," Desmond added.

"We've gone from bad to worse to unreal. This is a woman I called my sister and you're telling me she's a monster."

"She's worse than a monster," Desmond huffed. He was frustrated that he hadn't already found and killed her yet. "Do you think she pulled all this off on her own or does she have a partner?"

"I don't know. This is a woman I would've done anything for, but I have no idea who she even is. Desmond, let me be the one to handle Taren."

"Angel, I only told you about Taren as courtesy because we do business together and I respect your father. But I'ma need you to step back and stay out my way. Taren is a dead woman and there's nothing you can do about that."

"I'll respect your decision."

"Good because things are only about to get uglier. Taren crossed the line when she brought me into the fold. That's one move she'll live to regret," Desmond forewarned.

Nesa had been staying at a Motel 6 on the outskirts of Miami since fleeing her hotel room after getting that call from her cousin. She was blowing up TJ's phone, trying to figure out what happened to him. The next day while watching the six o'clock news all her questions were answered. Her cousin was found dead from a single gunshot in the hotel parking lot she had been staying at. Nesa knew she needed to get the hell out of town or she would be next. There was one major problem, the money Justina had given her was now gone. She had stashed the majority of the cash in the trunk of her car. She thought that was much safer than leaving it in her hotel room where a cleaning lady might decide to use her coins to retire early from her housekeeping job. The next day she went back to the hotel parking lot to retrieve her car and cash, but it was gone. She figured TJ's killer must've drove off with it.

Now Nesa was stuck in Miami with no money and a death sentence on her head. She felt she had no choice but to make contact with Angel and let her know what Justina hired her to do. Not only to expose Justina for her devious ways, but to also score a much needed payday. Her cousin died trying to protect her and she wanted to give him some form of justice.

"Hey, Clarissa, you got a second?"

"Nesa, where you been? Ain't nobody heard from you since the explosion. Are you coming back to work at the new club?"

"Nah. I'm done wit' Miami. Too much foul shit

going on here."

"So, you moving?"

"Yeah, I'm leaving town soon, but um before I go, I was hoping you could help me with something?"

"Help you with what?"

"I wanted to thank the woman who saved my life before I left town. Her name is Angel, but I don't know how to get in touch with her. Do you know anyone who might have her number?"

"Aspen worked for a woman named Angel. I wonder if it's the same woman," Clarissa said.

"Well, can you check around? I mean, it can't be but so many Angels that was at the club when the bomb went off. She also has a sister named Aaliyah who is engaged to Dale, the couple who the party was for that night."

"That's helpful. I'll track Angel down and let her know you're trying to get in touch with her."

"Thank you, Clarissa. Please hurry as I really need to get out of town soon."

"I'll do my best."

Nesa hung up with Clarissa and paced the floor in her seedy motel room. Her gut was telling her to forget about Justina, cut her losses, and get out of Miami, but she had grown to loathe that woman, especially now that TJ was dead. Justina might not have pulled the trigger, but Nesa placed the blame solely on her. She had to make Justina pay.

"Dirk, you are really trying my patience. You had me drive all the way over here to this dump, so you can tell me you haven't got shit done." Justina rolled her eyes in disgust.

"I apologize about my crib. I didn't have time to clean up," he said picking up some dirty paper plates and used plastic cups that were on the floor.

"I gave you forty-eight hours to get rid of Nesa. Those two days have turned into over a week. Not only that, you murdered her cousin in a fuckin' hotel parking lot. How stupid can you be?"

"The girly nigga tried to play me. He wasn't gonna take me to her. He was wasting my fuckin' time."

"You should've followed him to Nesa's room and waited for the right opportunity to take her down. Now, we have one man dead and the person you're supposed to be gunnin' for is nowhere to be found. So, who's wastin' who's fuckin' time?!" Justina spit.

"I get you pissed. I don't blame you, but I know I can find Nesa."

"For all you know, she could be long gone by now. I doubt she's still in Miami. Why would she be? By now she has to know her cousin is dead and you're responsible. You've put me in a fucked up predicament, Dirk. Now I have to clean up your mess," Justina complained.

"I can handle this... don't worry."

"I'm not because like I said, I'm going to clean up this mess, starting with you."

Justina pulled out her 44 Magnum and released two shots into Dirk's heart, killing him within a matter of seconds. She learned her lesson from Nesa... get rid of dead weight immediately. Before leaving, she took his phone and made sure there was nothing else linking him to her. When she ducked her head in his bedroom she noticed a small black bag on top of the dresser. Something told her to take a look inside.

"Well, well, well, what do we have here." Justina smiled, recognizing the envelopes full of cash she had given Nesa. "Dirk, yo' slick ass was trying to get paid twice. You somehow got ahold of the money I gave Nesa, then you were going to get paid again by me once you killed her. Too bad it didn't work out for you," Justina said out loud taking the money. With Dirk dead, the only thing left for Justina to do was find Nesa and get rid of her too.

Justina got into her non-descript rental car as she was aware a new model white Bentley would garner way too much attention, especially in this neighborhood. While pulling out the parking space she saw that Amir was calling her.

"Hey, baby! How are you?" Justina answered like she hadn't just killed a man less than five minutes ago.

"I'm good. Missing you, but I'll be in Miami next week for the wedding. I'm trying to arrive a couple days beforehand so I can spend some quality time with my beautiful, sexy girlfriend."

"That sounds perfect. As gorgeous as Miami is, it isn't the same without you."

"I'll do my best to make it happen. I miss seeing you and hearing your voice. I tried calling you a few times last night, but it kept going straight to voicemail."

"Sorry about that. I had a headache so I turned off my phone and went to bed early," she lied. Well, partially lied because Justina did go to bed early, but Desmond was right by her side.

"Are you feeling better?"

"I am, especially now that I've spoken to you."

"Good. I'm about to head into this meeting. I'll call you later on tonight. I love you."

"Love you, too."

When Justina got off the phone with Amir her mind immediately went to Desmond. She wasn't sure if it was the sexual chemistry, the physical attraction, his business savvy or a combination of all three, but Justina had fallen hard for Desmond.

What she believed would be a short summer fling until it was time to resume her life back in New York, had turned into so much more. Instead of trying to figure out a way to ruin Aaliyah's wedding, Justina's only concern was how to end her relationship with Amir so she could hold on to Desmond.

Chapter Twenty

Dirty Laundry

"I can't believe this is the final fitting before my wedding day," Aaliyah gushed, admiring herself in the mirror.

"You look gorgeous, Aaliyah!" Justina smiled.

"I agree, you really do," Angel chimed in.

"Thank you, but the two of you look absolutely beautiful in your maid of honor dresses. This might be way too much hotness for one wedding," Aaliyah joked.

"You're so silly. Are you nervous at all about tying the knot?" Angel asked.

"Were you?" Aaliyah asked right back.

"No."

"Neither am I. I'm marrying my soulmate. He accepts me for who I am and loves me unconditionally. As Justina definitely knows, and you Angel will quickly discover the more you're around me, I'm not exactly the easiest person to get along with," Aaliyah stated as if delighted by her admission.

"I can attest to that." Justina nodded.

"The point is, even with my colorful personality traits Dale adores me. And he isn't intimidated by my powerful family. He's his own man and I'm so proud that soon I'll be calling him my husband."

"Aaliyah, I really am so happy for you," Justina beamed. "You deserve to be happy," she said giving her a hug.

"And I am happy. The happiest I've ever been. In a few days, I'll be Mrs. Dale Clayborn. Maybe soon we'll be planning you and Amir's wedding," Aaliyah said smiling.

"Aaliyah, I need to speak with you for a minute," the wedding planner came into the store's private showroom and said.

"I'll be back shortly ladies," Aaliyah said, leaving the room.

"So, is Aaliyah right?"

"Right about what?" Justina stopped and asked Angel, before heading to one of the dressing rooms to take off her dress.

"About you and Amir. Should we be getting ready for wedding number two or are you saving yourself for Desmond?"

"Excuse me?! There's nothing going on between me and Desmond. We're just friends."

"I guess that's a good thing since Desmond seems to be very close to Dominique. He told me she's staying with him. Isn't that nice of Desmond to let one of his dancers stay with him while she's recuperating. She must be really special."

"From my understanding, they're not staying together, she's living at one of his apartments for the time being. And yes, you're right, that's very nice of Desmond." Justina was doing her best not to allow Angel to get under her skin, but it was proving difficult.

"Oh, is that what he told you? You know men, they love keeping secrets. But it doesn't concern you because you all are not sleeping with each other. Desmond is free to have sex with any woman he likes." Angel shrugged.

"Angel, do you have a problem with me?"

"Why would you say that?"

"Maybe because the few times we've been around each other, you always seem to throw shade my way. Although you keep it subtle, it doesn't go unnoticed."

"I'll be honest. There is something about you I don't like. Maybe it's because you're lying to Aaliyah and pretending to be in a loving relationship with Amir, but you're cheating on him with Desmond. And please don't insult my intelligence by denying it. I have a feeling that isn't the only secret you're keeping."

"Angel, let me give you some very valuable advice... mind your business. I know you're dying to fit in the family circle and be besties with your big sister, but Aaliyah has known you all of twenty-four hours. I suggest you fall back on trying to figure out who I'm having sex with. Don't pussy patrol me. I might start thinking you wanna taste me too," Justina smirked.

"You don't have to worry about that, you're not my type. I do suggest you watch your back because if you're hiding anything that will hurt my sister, Amir finding out that you're cheating on him will be the least of your worries."

"Angel, Angel, Angel... you are so out of your league coming for me," Justina ridiculed.

"I think it's the other way around. Yes, I do save lives, but I take them too."

Justina let out a haughty laugh. "You really are your father's child, but so am I. His name is T-Roc, you should do your research. Excuse me, I really need to get out of this dress. Now that everything is out in the open, I don't have to pretend it doesn't turn my stomach we're dressed alike."

Angel stood firm in her belief that Justina was a woman she needed to watch. Not only did she come off as disingenuous when it came to her friendship with Aaliyah, but she also sensed that Justina could be dangerous. Angel stepped out the room to make a necessary phone call.

"Hi, this is Angel. Call me back as soon as you get a moment. While you're searching for Taren, I have someone else I need you to investigate too."

After leaving a message for her private investigator, Angel was confident he would uncover any dirty laundry Justina wanted to keep hidden.

"Desmond, I'm so happy you came to see me. The lady you hired to take care of me is sweet, but we really don't have much to talk about." Dominique laughed. "It always seems she's watching my every move. Like she's my teacher and I'm in elementary school."

"Mrs. Armstrong only has your best interest."

"I know, but I feel like I'm suffocating. I'm ready

to get out again. Now that you reopened Diamonds & Pearls, I was thinking I can come back to work."

"Who told you I reopened the club?"

"I called Clarissa the other day and she told me."

"Dominique, I thought I made it clear you could only call family members."

"I know, but I was so lonely. I feel like I'm a prisoner. I just wanted to see what was going on in the real world." She sighed.

"I understand, but this is for your own protection. We haven't located Taren yet. You have round the clock security, but I don't want to take any chances."

"I didn't tell Clarissa where I was staying and even if I did, she wouldn't tell anyone." The grimace on Desmond's face let Dominique know he wasn't amused. "Please don't be upset with me. I promise I won't call her again until you say it's okay. But what about me going back to work?"

"Soon, but not right now. Whatever you need, I'll get it for you. You don't have to worry about money."

"Of course I want to start making my own money again, but it's not only that. I'm ready to get dressed, go out... feel alive again."

"I tell you what. I have a wedding I'm attending in a couple days, why don't you come as my date,"

Desmond suggested. "It will give you an opportunity to get dressed up, have your hair and makeup done. The best part, you'll be with me, so I'll know you're well protected."

"OMG!! That sounds amazing!! Thank you so much, Desmond!" Dominique ran up and gave him a huge hug. "This really means a lot to me. It's going to work wonders for my sanity."

"I love being able to put a smile on a woman's face, so I'm glad you're happy. I'll have a stylist come over later on today and you can pick out a dress you want to wear. The hair and makeup people will come Saturday morning, the day of the wedding. Sound good?"

"More like perfect. You saved me from that run-down strip club in Alabama and now you're saving me again. I don't know what I would do without you, Desmond."

"Get some rest. I'll call you in about an hour and let you know what time the stylist will be here."

"Okay, but do you have to leave so soon" Dominique asked, her voice full of displeasure.

"I'm meeting someone for lunch and I can't be late. But I'll see you on Saturday. Call me if you need me."

Dominique moped over to the door and locked it after Desmond left. She folded her arms, frowning her face, upset she couldn't convince him to stay longer.

"You like that man," Mrs. Armstrong came out of nowhere and said freaking Dominique out.

"I thought you left."

"I did, but I forgot something and had to come back and get it. Don't be embarrassed by what I said. If I was thirty years younger, I would like him too."

"Besides making sure I've eaten and taken my medicine, you never talk to me about anything. When you finally do say something, it's about Desmond." Dominique shook her head with annoyance and headed towards the kitchen to get a glass a juice.

"I didn't mean to upset you, Dominique. I made an observation and commented on it. Mr. Blackwell is quite a catch. I doubt a man like that will stay single very long. So, if you want him, you better make your move to get him. That's some free advice from a much older woman who has lived a very full life." Mrs. Armstrong winked, leaving back out.

Dominique wasn't ready to admit to Mrs. Armstrong or anyone else, but she couldn't deny it to herself. She was enamored with Desmond. He was everything she always wanted in a man, but didn't think she could have. She was sure he cared about her as a friend, now Dominique had to convince him they could be much more than that. Although she didn't appreciate Mrs. Armstrong budding into her business, she did give Dominique the push she needed to go after what she wanted and that was Desmond Blackwell.

"Normally, I'm the one who's always late. If feels good being the one on time," Justina said when Desmond sat down.

"I apologize, but I had to stop and pick up something," he said holding up a small bag. "Have you ordered yet?"

"No, I was waiting for you."

"I've never been here before, but this place is impressive," he commented, glancing around at the pristine white décor with the sweeping draperies that would lure anyone in that was in the mood for Italian cuisine.

'The food is delicious too. I remember you mentioning your weakness for pasta. You will love their Truffle Tagliatelle. It's handmade pasta, seasonal truffle, and cream. Perfection."

"I'm sold. Before I forget, this is what I had to pick up." Desmond lifted up the bag and took out a black velvet box. "This is for you."

Justina's eyes widened with awe at the 40.00ct natural princess cut, ruby and white diamond, three row bracelet.

"I'm speechless."

"Put it on. I thought you could wear it to Aaliyah's wedding."

"It will look incredible with the maid of honor dress I'm wearing. You're amazing. Thank you, baby." Justina leaned over and kissed Desmond. "I wish we were going to the wedding together."

"I do, too. Hold on one second, I have to take this call."

Justina continued to admire the extravagant piece of jewelry Desmond had gifted her with. It looked regal on her wrist. She wasn't paying any attention to his phone conversation until she heard him mention styling his date for a wedding and then giving whoever he was speaking to an address which Justina made a notation of. She waited for Desmond to end his call and then Justina went in with her interrogation.

"Did I hear you correctly? You're bringing a date to Aaliyah's wedding?"

"Dominique is getting restless being stuck in the apartment. I'm taking her to the wedding so she can get some fresh air."

"She can go stand on the balcony if she needs some fresh air. I'm sure the apartment you have her staying at has one," Justina snapped.

"She hasn't been able to go out for weeks. Having her come with me to a wedding isn't a big deal."

"Yes, it is!" Justina banged her hand down on the table.

"Calm down," Desmond said, noticing patrons dining at the restaurant turning in their direction

"You're bringing one of your strippers as a date to my best friend's wedding and you're telling me to calm down. How dare you!"

"Who's coming to the wedding with you?" Desmond countered.

"That's different. I was with Amir before I even knew you."

"Amir? Genesis's son, Amir, is your man?"

"Yes, why?"

"He came to my office with Nico a few weeks ago. I didn't know he was your man."

"You never asked and why does it matter, it doesn't change anything. What you're doing is completely disrespectful."

"Disrespectful to who? Nobody even knows we're seeing each other," Desmond scoffed.

"I know," she yelled. "Don't my feelings matter."

"Do mine... huh? You let me lay up in the bed next to you every night. Touching you, kissing you, making love to you every which way. Giving your body to me and in a couple of days you'll be doing the same fuckin' thing with another man. That's what you call disrespectful," Desmond stood up and said, then walked out.

"Desmond!" Justina yelled, but he kept walking right out the door.

Chapter Twenty-One

That Man Is Mine

"Coming!" Dominique called out, rushing to open the door. "Hi! You must be the stylist Desmond hired to dress me for the wedding," she said cheerfully.

"I'm not the stylist and you're not the little lady of the house," Justina popped, brushing past an alarmed Dominique.

"Oh gosh, did Taren send you?"

"Who the hell is Taren?!"

"What do you want and why are you here?"

"I'm sure your, 'I'm so scared, please save me' act works wonders on Desmond, but all it's doing is pissing me off."

"You know Desmond?" Dominique's voice cracked.

Justina stared at the petite beauty in her cut off shorts and fitted tank top. It was all in her eyes and even the way she said his name, she was smitten with Desmond.

"Yes, I know Desmond, very well," she stressed. "Whatever you think is happening or is gonna happen with Desmond, it's not. He's with me." Justina pointed her well-manicured finger in Dominique's face.

"If Desmond is with you, then why am I going to be his date for a wedding on Saturday?" Dominique had a smug glare on her face. She thought about what Mrs. Armstrong told her earlier that day. Dominique had no plans giving up on Desmond so easily.

"You're nothing more than a charity case. Men like Desmond love finding wounded little birdies on the side of the road and nursing them back to health. Once you're all fixed up, he'll open up that window and send you on your way. Fly little birdie, fly," Justina taunted, flipping her hand.

"I think you need to leave. I'm expecting the stylist Desmond hired to dress me for our date," Dominique twisted her neck and sniped.

"Sweetheart, I can afford my own stylist to dress me, although I don't need one. While you're bragging about Desmond spending a few dollars so you can leave the house with him looking halfway decent, he's lacing me with gifts like this." Justina damn near shoved her iced out wrist down Dominique's throat.

"Get your hand outta my face!" Dominique barked, slapping Justina's arm away.

Without thinking, Justina shoved Dominique, pushing her down on the hardwood floor. She was about to start stomping her with the heel of her shoe, but regained her composure and exercised some self-control.

"Get out!" Dominique roared.

"I'll leave, but you need to get your shit together. The quicker you stop acting like a hapless puppy, the sooner Desmond can dismiss yo' ass." Justina slit her eyes at Dominique, before slamming the door shut as she left the building.

"I'm not going anywhere!" Dominique shouted even though Justina was long gone. "If that spiteful broad believes I'm just gonna hand him over to her, she is underestimating me. Desmond clearly isn't hers yet and if I have my way, he never will be."

Dominique's heartbeat was rapid and her breathing heavy. Justina came through like a storm, disrupting the fairytale life she was beginning to create in her mind with Desmond. But she wouldn't be discouraged. The only thing Justina accomplished by showing up was becoming Dominique's ultimate motivation to do whatever necessary to get her man.

"Mr. Blackwell, your assistant said you wanted to see me."

"Yes. Close the door and have a seat, Clarissa."

Clarissa was nervous as hell. She still remembered feeling like she was going to come up missing after Desmond didn't appreciate the tone she took with him. She had learned better and came in being polite from the jump.

"How can I help you, Mr. Blackwell?"

"Dominique told me she spoke with you the other day."

"Yes, she did call me. I was happy to hear from her because I was worried. I wanted to make sure she was okay."

"Physically and mentally Dominique is doing much better. But she still might be in danger so I didn't want her speaking to anyone other than her family."

"I understand, but I would never do anything that might jeopardize Dominique's safety."

"I believe you wouldn't do anything purposely, but things happen. To play it safe, I don't want you mentioning to anyone you've spoken to Dominique. Are we clear?"

"Yes, I won't say a thing to anyone. Can I ask you something?"

"Sure, what is it?"

"Are you any closer to finding out who killed Aspen?"

"I know the two of you were very close. I'm hopeful we're closer to finding the individual who killed Aspen and when we do, I'll let you know."

"Thank you. If there isn't anything else, can I go now?"

"Yes, you can go."

"Before I forget," Clarissa stopped mid-stride and turned to Desmond. "Nesa, who used to work at the other Diamonds & Pearls—"

"What about her?"

"She's moving out of state and wanted to thank Angel for saving her life that night at the club before she left. I remember Aspen mentioning you and Angel are business partners."

"True."

"Would you ask her to call Nesa? It would mean a lot to Nesa to personally thank Angel for saving her life."

"I'm sure it would. Give me Nesa's phone number and I'll pass it along to Angel. I'm sure she would like to speak to Nesa also."

"Thank you so much, Mr. Blackwell," Clarissa enthused, writing Nesa's phone number down on a piece of paper and handing it to Desmond.

"Don't worry, I'll be happy to take care of this for you."

Desmond glanced down at the paper. When he reopened the club, Nesa was one of the dancers they reached out to but the number on file was disconnected. He wondered what happened to her as she hustled hard in the club. Now that he had her new number, Desmond decided he would personally give her a call to find out why she was leaving town and not coming back to dance at the club.

"Baby this is the last day we're going to spend together before I check into my hotel suite tomorrow," Aaliyah said, nuzzling Dale's neck. "I think we should stay in bed all day and make love."

"That sounds mad sexy, but I'ma be the bigger person and say, let's wait and make love again on our honeymoon. I know we ain't virgins, but we can make it seem like the first time if we throw a break in between now and then." Dale laughed but was dead serious.

"You play too much!" Aaliyah grabbed one of the decorative pillows off the bed and hit Dale over the head. "You know damn well you don't wanna wait." Aaliyah began kissing on her fiancé, getting him worked up.

"Nope! I'm not gonna let this happen." Dale jumped out the bed.

"Where you going?"

"Take a shower, get dressed, and handle my business. I'll be a married man come Saturday. I wanna make sure our wedding day is impeccable."

"It will be. I know you're going to look delicious wearing your tux and wait until you see me in my dress. Babe, it's flawless. You'll be rushing to get me on that private jet, so we can do all sorts of nasty things, but this time as husband and wife." Aaliyah giggled.

"I can't wait." Dale smiled.

"Me neither." Aaliyah glided her naked body over to Dale who was standing in the entrance leading to the bathroom. He thought she was about to give him a kiss, but instead she knelt down and swallowed all his manhood with her wet lips and then stopped.

"I'll finish on our wedding night," Aaliyah teased, leaving her soon-to-be husband with a rock hard dick and nowhere to put it.

Chapter Twenty-Two

Damaged

Justina was in the process of taking her clothes off so she could take a long hot bubble bath when she heard someone at the door. She debated if she should answer due to her stressful day.

"Open up, Justina!" Desmond shouted loudly banging on the door. "I know you in there. I can hear the music," he continued to shout.

"What is it?!" she asked, opening the door wearing nothing, but her lace thong.

"I know you ain't in here wit' some other nigga!" Desmond barked, brushing past Justina.

"I'm home alone. I was about to take a bath," she said closing the door. I haven't heard from you since you left me at the restaurant sitting alone. Why show up now?"

"What were you thinking going to see Dominique and threatening her?"

"Oh, is that what she told you," Justina said in her most condescending voice.

"Yeah, because that's what you did."

"And you know this to be true because your precious little girlfriend would never lie to you." Justina reached for her glass of wine on the table already over the conversation before it even had a real chance to get started.

"I know it to be true because of the type of person you are."

"Honestly, I don't care what you think about me anymore, Desmond. Go be with your needy, whiny girlfriend and leave me the hell alone. I promise not to ever bother you or her again," Justina scoffed, swallowing the rest of her wine then pouring herself another glass. "You can see yourself out. You know your way to the front door. I'm going to take my bubble bath and relax. Have a good life, Desmond."

Justina's dismissive attitude had Desmond reeling. When she turned her back on him, he lunged at her. "You think you can walk away from me!"

"That's what I was doing wasn't I... walking away. Kinda like how you did me at the restaurant."

"Everything is tic for tac with you. Maybe I should walk out that door and not look back because you bring out this part of me that I don't like."

"By all means get to steppin'," Justina mimicked. "I'm positive Dominique is waiting for you with open arms. "

"Yeah, I'm sure she is. Dominique might be more my type. I need a real woman who knows how to act, instead of a silly chick like you."

"Fuck you!" Justina wailed. Tossing her wine in Desmond's face. "I hate you!" she kept screaming over and over again.

"No, you don't," Desmond said pinning her against the wall. "You hate that you love me."

"Just go. Why don't you just leave me alone." Justina's attitude was a mixture of anger and pain.

"Because I can't. Everything inside of me knows I should, but I can't."

Like two magnets you cannot pull away, Desmond and Justina began kissing each other with their typical intensity and passion. They were drawn to each other in a way no one could explain. It was intoxicating.

"I want you to be mine. All mine and no one else's," Desmond stated between their obsessive exchanges of kisses.

"I'm scared to give all of myself to you," Justina's admission stunned her and made Desmond stop what he was doing. "I didn't mean to say that." She tried to take it back, but it was too late.

"But you did. What are you scared of?" He forced Justina to look him in the eyes. She tried her best to fight it, but she was no match to his strength. "Tell me what you're scared of," Desmond demanded.

"If you knew the things that I've done and what I'm capable of, you really would walk away and I'd lose you forever."

"Tell me."

"Tell you what?" she asked.

"Tell me everything you've done. Tell me what made a woman like you, who has everything, become so insecure and scared. I wanna know."

"I can't tell you... I can't." Sadness and shame came over Justina's face.

"Yes, you can."

"No, I can't. You'll think I'm a monster and you would probably be right."

"If you were truly a monster, I wouldn't see remorse in your eyes."

Justina stepped away from Desmond, needing to put some distance between them.

"I wish I never let myself fall in love with you." Justina meant that too. For the last few years, every calculated move she made was driven by hate and revenge. Falling in love was never part of her plan. It made her tap into emotions she buried so deep, Justina didn't even realize they still existed until now.

"It's too late for all that because I'm in love with you, too."

"You say that now, but once I tell you everything, I doubt your feelings for me will be the same."

"Let me decide," Desmond said, leading Justina over to the sofa so they could sit down.

Justina dreaded having this conversation with Desmond. But part of her was ready to unleash all these secrets she had been carrying around. It was better for her to be honest with him so he could walk away now instead of falling even deeper in love and Desmond walking away later.

"I'll tell you, but you have to promise me one thing."

"What is it?"

"No matter what happens between us, you can never use what I'm about to tell you against me or share the information with anyone else. Can you promise me that?"

"I promise," Desmond agreed.

With his promise, Justina sat stoically and shared every dark detail, starting from the very beginning. She didn't sugarcoat a thing, revealing every murder she committed, every scam she'd been a part of, even her affiliation with Maya. Desmond listened intently without interrupting unless he needed clarification on one of the deeds she was discussing. An hour turned into two and two turned into three. By the time Justina finally finished purging her soul, she was astounded by all the dirt she'd done. She only could imagine what Desmond thought of her.

"You're so quiet. I did give you a lot to process. You're probably overwhelmed."

"I am. I figured what you had to say was bad, but not this bad. To make matters worse, a lot of this stuff is recent. Like murdering Dirk after hiring him to kill Nesa, and her cousin ending up dead in the process." Desmond got up from the sofa, frustrated. "Then Markell. He was a good dude. He loved you. You took him out all because he wanted you to end this vendetta against Aaliyah and Amir. Your hate for them is destroying your life and the lives of innocent people."

"The damage is done. There's nothing I can do to change it."

"What about your situation with Aaliyah. Trying to use the information about her father killing Emory to end their engagement. I guess it was a blessing in disguise that Dale suffered the head injury in the explosion so he wouldn't remember what Nesa told him. But you still know. Are you planning to find a shrewd way to drop that bomb before the wedding?"

"Honestly, I've become so fixated on getting rid of Nesa, I put doing any damage to Aaliyah and Dale's wedding on the backburner," Justina acknowledged.

"Got it. So, you haven't given up on ruining their lives. After you kill Nesa, you'll get back to Aaliyah. Do you even hear yourself? There's no voice of reason in your head. And your relationship with Amir. Do you care about him at all?"

"He was my first love. But then he started seeing my best friend behind my back. At first, I blamed Aaliyah. I thought if she hadn't kept throwing herself at Amir they would've never gotten together. Then I realized he was just as culpable. All I wanted to do was make Amir fall in love with me and then break his heart. It was going smoothly until I met you."

"You're a changed woman... I seriously doubt that."

"You're right. I haven't changed. There is only one thing different about me."

"What's that?"

"I'm in love with you. I know you can feel it."

"Do you love me enough to stop this madness?" Desmond asked.

"Yes, but it doesn't matter. It's too late."

"Why do you say it's too late?"

"Because Nesa is determined to get in contact

with Angel and let her know what I had her do. Once that happens, it'll turn into a domino effect. Angel and Aaliyah will try to uncover every skeleton in my closet."

"I'll take care of Nesa."

"I don't know where she is though," Justina told him.

"Don't worry about that. Like I said, I'll take care of Nesa."

"Does that mean you're not gonna leave me?"

"It means I'm giving you one last chance to get your life together. No more of this bullshit. No more blaming Amir and Aaliyah for everything that's gone wrong in your life. All this vindictiveness ends today. If you can't do that, then I'm done. I'm wiping my hands of you. I won't tell anybody what you told me, but I don't ever wanna see your face again," Desmond made clear.

"I'll change, I promise. Whatever you want me to do. I'll do it. I don't wanna lose you," Justina held on to Desmond and pleaded.

"The first thing you're gonna do is end your relationship with Amir."

"I don't have a problem with that. I don't love Amir. I'll tell him it's over as soon as he gets in town."

"I also want you to get help."

"What sort of help?"

"See a psychiatrist," Desmond stated. "I know

that's taboo to a lot of people, but Justina you need help... professional help."

"You do think I'm some sort of monster that only a doctor can fix."

"I don't think you're a monster but you're severely damaged. I can't help you if you're not willing to help yourself."

Justina sat down on a barstool and put her head down. "My mother was put into a mental facility after she killed a man and accidently shot me. Before you even ask, I'll tell you that story another time. I'm only bringing this up because I don't believe those places work. My mother faked her way through it. I do believe she's changed, but I don't believe it had anything to do with her getting professional help."

"I don't know your mom's situation or what facility she went to, but I know a doctor that is excellent at what she does. All I'm asking is you be open to try. I'm not willing to try and make our relationship work if you don't do this."

"Basically, either I get professional help or you're done with me. You're not giving me much of a choice."

"You always have a choice, which one are you choosing?"

"I choose you," Justina looked up and said.

"Good choice."

Justina got up and went over to Desmond,

wrapping her arms around him tightly. For the first time in her life, she loved a man who she was able to completely reveal herself to and he still loved her too. But would Desmond's love be enough for Justina to end her cold, calculating, and deadly ways.

Nesa was parked at Diamonds & Pearls waiting for Clarissa. She was smoking nervously in the cheap, used car she recently purchased with the last few dollars she had left to get out of town. Nesa called the club to see what shift Clarissa was working that night, but per usual she was late.

"Finally, there she go!" Nesa tossed her Newport on the ground, putting it out with her shoe. She rushed over, trying to catch her before she went in the club.

"Clarissa!" Nesa yelled.

Clarissa heard her name and turned around to see who it was, but was thrown off by Nesa's appearance.

"It's me, Nesa."

"Girl, why are you dressed like that?" Clarissa was used to seeing Nesa with her twenty inch laid weaves, five-inch heels, form-fitting clothes, and a face full of Milani makeup. But this Nesa had her weave in a messy bun with a bandana tied around the front, jeans, t-shirt with converse, huge sunglasses that practically covered her entire face and some Vaseline on her lips.

"I told you I was moving so I been packing," she stammered, biting her nails.

"Are you okay? You don't look too good," Clarissa said, concerned.

"I've been trying to reach you. Why haven't you called me back?"

"I went out of town to work this gig at this private party. It was paying extra and I needed the money. When I got back I was tired. I was gonna call you tonight when I got off work. Why what's up?"

"Did you ever get in touch with Angel?"

"No, but I spoke to Desmond."

"Why you speak to Desmond... what he got to do wit' it?"

"I remembered that Aspen told me Desmond was business partners with Angel. Who would be better to relay your message than him?"

"So, did you give him my number?" Nesa wanted to know.

"Yeah, I did. Maybe he hasn't talked to her yet or maybe this Angel chick hasn't gotten around to calling you yet." Clarissa shrugged.

"Is Desmond in his office?"

"I haven't been inside yet, but I'm sure he is.

Why?"

"I'ma go talk to him. Find out if he gave Angel my message," Nesa said, about to walk towards the club entrance.

"Wait!" Clarissa grabbed Nesa's arm. "I don't think you should go in Desmond's office looking like that. You know how that nigga is. He gon' look at you like you crazy," she warned.

Nesa thought about what Clarissa said and she was right. Nesa was broke, on edge, and she looked it. She rarely left the rundown motel she was staying at and wasn't getting any sleep because she was scared someone was going to show up and kill her.

"Nesa, I understand you want to thank this woman for saving your life, but I'm sure it will be fine if you tell her over the phone, instead of staying in town so you can tell her in person."

"No, I need to see her. I wanna thank her and talk to her about Justina."

"Who is Justina?" Clarissa gave her a perplexed stare, but Nesa wasn't paying attention. Her mind was somewhere else.

"I gotta go. I'll come back later to see Desmond," Nesa said rushing off.

"Damn, that shit was strange," Clarissa said, heading inside. Before getting ready for work, Clarissa decided to stop by Desmond's office to ask him if he had gotten in touch with Angel. Nesa's behavior and appearance had Clarissa rattled. If linking her up with Angel could help Nesa's cause then she would try her best to make it happen.

As Clarissa got closer to Desmond's office, she noticed his assistant was talking to a woman that had on some shoes that she knew for a fact cost a pretty penny.

"I spoke to Desmond and told him I was dropping off this paperwork. He told me he wasn't coming in until later and to leave it with you."

"Thanks, Angel," she said taking the envelope. "I'll make sure Mr. Blackwell gets it."

"Great!"

"Just my luck!" Clarissa exclaimed, following Angel as she was walking off. "Can I speak to you for a minute?"

"Sure, what can I do for you?" Angel stopped and asked.

"A friend of mine named Nesa has been trying to get in touch with you."

"Nesa... that name sounds very familiar."

"You saved her life during the club explosion," Clarissa reminded Angel.

"Yes! That's where I know the name from. How is she doing?"

"She's doing okay. She was just here. Nesa's moving out of town, but before leaving she really wanted to speak to you. She wanted to thank you in person for saving her life."

"That's so sweet." Angel smiled.

"Please take her number," Clarissa said writing it down on a napkin. "It would mean so much to her if you called. I don't think she's going to leave town until you do."

"I'll call her as soon as I get in my car," Angel promised.

"Great and by the way, I love your shoes!" Clarissa gushed before hurrying off to get ready for work.

"Thanks!" Keeping her promise, Angel started dialing Nesa's number while headed to her car.

"Hello."

"Hi, is this Nesa?"

"Who wants to know?" she asked suspiciously.

"This is Angel. A friend of yours gave me your number."

"Angel! I've been trying to get in touch with you."

"So, I heard. How are you? Are you feeling okay since the explosion?"

"Yeah, I'm much better. Thanks so much for asking."

"Of course. I've thought about you a lot since that night. I'm glad you're doing okay."

"Yes, I really wanted to thank you for saving my life. Talking to you, you sound so sweet, I feel like shit for what I'm about to say, but I'm desperate."

"What are you about to say?" Angel closed her car door. She waited to hear what Nesa had to say before starting the engine.

"I have some information that I know you would want to hear."

"Okay, tell me."

"The thing is I'm trying to get out of town and I need some money to make that happen."

"So, what you want me to pay you for this information?"

"Yes, but I really do need the money and it will be worth the price."

"Tell you what, share with me what you know and if I find it valuable, I'll pay you whatever price you want," Angel said.

"How do I know after I give you the info you'll come through with the money?" Nesa questioned.

"Because I'm a woman of my word."

"I really don't have a choice at this point, but can we meet in person? That way, after you hear what I have to say, you can hand over my money so I can get the hell out of town."

"You sound awfully confident that I'll want to pay you for whatever you have to say."

"I am, so bring a lot of cash," Nesa stated.

"Give me a little hint of what I can expect. I need to calculate a number in my head before we meet."

"It's regarding Justina and something she had me do to your sister Aaliyah."

"How soon can we meet?" Angel asked with the quickness.

"Give me an hour. I'll text you with the location."

"I'll be there," Angel said without hesitation and she planned on bringing plenty of money. She prayed the information Nesa had would be what she needed to expose Justina for the evil woman she believed her to be.

Chapter Twenty-Three

Circle Of Drama

"My apologies, I hope I didn't interrupt anything. I didn't realize you had company," Aaliyah said when she entered Dale's office.

"You don't have to apologize, babe." Dale came from behind his desk and walked over to Aaliyah.

"You know Owen and Randy. These other guys are some friends of mine in town for our wedding."

"Nice... hello everyone." Aaliyah waved. "Well, I'm not going to keep you, baby. I just wanted to say bye before I left for the hotel. Next time you see me, I'll be walking down the aisle."

"I can't wait."

"Me neither, my love." Aaliyah kissed Dale goodbye. Saturday couldn't get here fast enough for her.

"Where the hell is she?" Angel mumbled looking at her watch. She tried calling Nesa again, but this time it went straight to voicemail. Angel glanced down at the bag full of money she was carrying. She was prepared to give Nesa every dollar if it was worth it. Angel even brought an extra bonus if the information was juicy enough. Now, here she sat with no Nesa in sight.

Angel waited for another hour at the restaurant by the beach they agreed to meet at. She was sitting outside on the patio scrutinizing every person that walked by and every car driving down the street. It baffled her what could keep Nesa away. She sounded so desperate on the phone for money, yet she was a no-show. Angel began to wonder if Nesa was playing some sort of game and at the last minute bailed because she knew she couldn't deliver the goods.

"Let me call this chick one last time," Angel

huffed. Once again, the call when straight to voicemail. "I can't believe this chick wasted my damn
time!" Angel grabbed her bag of money and bolted.

"Desmond, I wasn't expecting to see you until
Saturday. But of course, I'm always happy to see
you." Dominique's entire face lit up.

"I'm happy to see you, too."

"Come take a look at the dress I decided to
wear for the wedding. It's a beautiful silk material
in a light pink color."

"Dominique, I came over to speak to you about
that."

"About my dress?"

"No, the wedding. I'm not going to be able to
take you."

"Why not?" Dominique let out a long sigh.
"Does this have to do with the woman who stopped
by yesterday?"

"Yes."

"Is she your girlfriend?"

'Yes, she is."

"Why did you invite me to this wedding if you
have a girlfriend."

"I never meant to put you in the middle of this.

My relationship with Justina is complicated."

"Let me ask you something... why her? I mean, she's beautiful and all in that superficial way. But you're nothing like that, at least that's what I thought. How can someone like you be with someone like her?"

"I'll be the first to admit, Justina has some issues that need to be addressed, but I love her and I'm committed to helping her work through it."

"I guess that means you're putting me out and I can no longer stay here."

"No! I want you to stay here until I know you're safe. After that, once you get back to work, you can continue to stay here or I can help you get a place of your own. I still consider you a friend, Dominique. That hasn't changed," Desmond made clear. "I hope you still consider me to be a friend too."

"I do. You're a good man, Desmond. Better than any man I've ever known."

"Thank you. Listen, I have to go, but nothing has changed. If you need anything, you're always free to call me. Don't forget that."

"I won't." Dominique wanted to run in the bedroom, close the door, and cry her heart out when Desmond left. She fantasized about them starting this whole life together and it was shattered in a matter of minutes. But even with Desmond now claiming Justina as his girl and disinviting her to the wedding, Dominique would not be deterred. She believed Desmond deserved a much better woman than Justina and that she was the perfect fit. Now all Dominique had to do was convince Desmond.

It was the night before her wedding and Aaliyah was lying her head down on the 18ᵗʰ century Japanese silk pillows in her hotel suite. The room offered 360-degree floor to ceiling views, which she could see from the comfort of her bed. She was watching an old episode of "SVU" on a Bang & Olufsen BeoVision 103-inch plasma TV when she heard the door.

"That must be Amir," she said putting the remote down.

"Here comes the bride!" Amir smiled when Aaliyah opened the door wearing her I can't keep calm I'm getting married cotton pajama set.

"Isn't it crazy, I'll be a married woman tomorrow... who would've thought." She laughed, letting Amir in.

"A year ago, I wouldn't have believed it, but seeing you now, you're ready. You're going to be an amazing wife, Aaliyah."

"Thank you!" she hugged Amir. "Just think a few years ago I thought you would be the man I'd marry."

"Now you're marrying Dale and I'll be marrying Justina."

"Wait! You proposed to Justina?"

"Not yet, but…"

"But you plan on proposing?" Aaliyah cut Amir off and asked.

"I mean I've known Justina for most of my life. We've been through more than a lot of married couples. She's been my best friend and we've been close to enemies, but yet we survived it. Now we're in love. I can't imagine another woman I should marry."

"Yeah, the three of us have all changed so much. We used to be inseparable growing up. Justina was the sweet one, I was the spoiled, sassy one, and you were the cocky, annoying one," she cracked.

"Besides Justina and me, you're pretty much the same," Amir joked. "I'm kidding. You've grown into a wonderful woman and Dale is a very lucky man."

"So is Justina. She's my best friend and I couldn't have picked a better man for her."

"Thanks… how could I forget, this is for you," Amir said handing Aaliyah a present.

"I was wondering who that was for."

"It's actually from my dad. He and my mom are still out of the country on vacation. He regrets that he's not able to be here, but he ordered this gift for you and had me pick it up from the jewelry store."

"Jewelry... nice!" Aaliyah beamed. "I can't wait to open it. But I'll save it for my wedding day."

"Let me get outta here. I came straight from the airport to see you and Justina's waiting on me."

"Thank you for stopping by, Amir. It was really nice spending time with you. It felt like old times. I know I'ma be a married woman, like tomorrow, but I hope we'll still make time to be in each other's lives."

"Always." They embraced for a hug before Amir left.

Aaliyah felt a tinge of sadness as Amir walked out the door. It was like she was saying goodbye to her past one last time, but smiled as she looked forward to her future with Dale.

"I'm finding it hard to believe tomorrow I'll be walking Aaliyah down the aisle. I wish I could've done the same with you, Angel," Nico said pouring himself a drink.

"I do too, but having you in my life makes up for all of that."

"You're such an amazing young lady. I never had a chance to meet Lisa's mother, but she had to be an incredible woman because she did such an amazing job with you," Nico stated proudly.

"My grandmother was pretty terrific. She did her best to make me feel my mother's presence even though she was dead. I wish growing up I had you and my mother in my life, but I feel so blessed my grandmother stepped up. She gave me all the love she had."

"I can tell. I wasn't there for you growing up, but I will be there for my grandkids. Because you're going to make one hell of a mother."

"Slow down, Dad! Darien and I haven't even been married for a year yet. I wanna take my time with having kids. I might've been first to get married, but I think Aaliyah will be first to be a mother."

"I swear I never thought I would live to see Aaliyah get married. She's always been so carefree." Nico smiled adoringly. "I love that girl to death, but she's a handful. I commend Dale because I didn't think any man would be able to get her to settle down." Nico let out a loud chuckle. "At one point, I thought Amir might've had a chance but that didn't work out."

"Aaliyah and Amir dated?" this was news to Angel.

"Yes. They seemed to be in love."

"This must've been before he started dating Justina."

"Amir was actually with Justina first then he started dating Aaliyah... you know how kids do. It did get very messy, make that ugly. But it worked out the way it's supposed to. Aaliyah is marrying Dale. Amir and Justina are back together."

"Interesting. What is your take on Justina?" Angel inquired.

"Her and Aaliyah have been friends since they were little girls. Justina always looked up to Aaliyah but as they got older that admiration turned into jealousy once Aaliyah and Amir started dating behind Justina's back and then hatred."

"Really, sounds like it got pretty bad."

"Worse than bad. Aaliyah ended up going to jail because of Justina and her mother." Nico put his drink down becoming upset reliving that time in their lives.

"Jail?! What in the world did they do?"

"Justina's crazy ass mother, Chantal, killed that rapper Sway and accidentally shot her own daughter."

"Oh gosh, I recall hearing about Sway getting killed when I was in middle school. I had no idea they were the players in that drama."

"Baby girl, this circle you in now is nothing but drama. There's not enough days in the year for me to tell you all the drama we've dealt with individually and collectively."

"I guess the longer I'm around the more I'll learn."

"True indeed, but why the questions about Justina?"

"Remember that woman I pulled out the club the night of the explosion?"

"Yeah, I remember, what about her?"

"I got a call from her. First, she thanked me for saving her life and then she told me she had information about Justina hiring her to do something to Aaliyah," Angel told Nico.

"Do something to Aaliyah like what?" Nico put his drink down and leaned forward in his chair.

"That's the thing, we were supposed to meet for her to tell me, but she never showed up."

"Why couldn't she just tell you on the phone?"

"Because she wanted me to pay her for the info. She's trying to move out of Miami and needed the money."

Nico scowled up his face and was shaking his head before getting up to pour himself another drink.

"I know it seems iffy, but she sounded legit on the phone," Angel tried to reason.

"Then why she ain't show up?"

"I can't figure that out either." Angel sighed.

"Listen, both Justina and Aaliyah have very high profile, famous fathers. Not sure if you know this but Justina's dad is T-Roc and of course you know about Supreme. There will always be opportunists spreading lies, trying to make a quick buck off them because of that. That's what this woman sounds like. Justina had issues in the past, but she seems to have turned her life around and be on the right track."

"I'm sure you're right."

"Don't waste your time on this bullshitin' ass people," Nico said as he swung his arm. "Let that shit go."

"Don't worry, Dad, I'm letting it go," Angel lied. She had no plans of dismissing her ill feelings towards Justina. Angel considered Nesa not showing up a minor setback. Her gut instinct told her Justina was up to no good and Angel planned to keep digging until it was confirmed.

Chapter Twenty-Four

The Wedding

"Aaliyah, I can't put into words how beautiful you look." Precious stared at her first-born child wearing a white pearl embroidery, hand-stitched silk and satin custom-designed wedding dress and she could not hold back her tears.

"Mommy, please don't cry. This is supposed to be the no tear zone... remember!"

Mother and daughter both laughed.

"I can't help but to cry. Looking at you in your

wedding dress reminds me of the day I married Supreme. You know I was only a teenager when I married your father. His mother couldn't stand me. Even though she'll never admit it, she still can't." Precious laughed.

"You're so silly. Grandma likes you. Don't tell her I told you, but right before you came in, she was here. She said, 'You look just like your mother did on her wedding day to my son, simply beautiful.'" Aaliyah smiled.

"She really said that?"

"Yep! But she told me if I ever repeated it to anyone, including you, she would deny it." Aaliyah giggled.

"Sounds like her. But she's right, you look simply beautiful. Dale is going to lose his mind when he sees you walking down the aisle."

"I hope so. I love him so much, Mom."

"I know you do. I can see it in your eyes."

"I never thought I would find a man who would love me unconditionally, but I did. I feel so blessed."

"This is a new beginning to the rest of your life. I feel honored that I can share this wonderful day with you," Precious said lovingly. "I wanna kiss you all over your gorgeous face so bad, but I refuse to mess up your makeup. But I can at least hold you one last time as my baby girl, before you become a married woman."

"I can't wait to get you out of that dress," Desmond whispered in Justina's ear while they were standing in front of the glass double doors that led out to the illuminated 20-foot lake fountain.

"I can't wait either, baby." Justina softly kissed him on the lips.

"You never answered my question," Desmond said kissing her neck.

"What question?"

"How did it go with Amir?"

"About that." Justina was reluctant to tell Desmond, but she knew how persistent he was. "By the time Amir got to my place I was sleep. Then I had to wake up early and meet Aaliyah at her hotel. I've only talked to him on the phone briefly."

"So, you haven't told Amir. Are you playing me, Justina?"

"No!" Justina held Desmond's jaw and turned it to face her. "I love you. You're the last person I would try to play. I want us to be together. I promise, I'm going to tell Amir." Justina kissed Desmond one more time. "The wedding is about to start so I have to go, but I love you... only you."

Angel watched as Justina hurried off and then

made a beeline to Desmond.

"Don't you think you're being a little reckless? Her man could've seen the two of you."

"Angel, we're business partners. My personal life doesn't concern you."

"Do you have feelings for her? I mean, yeah she's easy on the eyes, but you're way too smart to fall for a woman like that."

"A woman like what?"

"Manipulative, dangerous, and clearly a cheater."

"You're out of line, Angel. Justina and I are in a relationship... she's my woman and when you talk about her like that, I find it very disrespectful."

"Your woman?! Does Amir know about this or is it still your's and Justina's dirty little secret?"

"I'm 'bout to go take my seat and get ready for the ceremony to start. I like having you as a business partner in Angel's Girls, let's not ruin that because you don't know how to mind your business. Now excuse me."

"There you are! You said you'd be right back, then you disappeared." Aaliyah was happy to see Angel as she was ready to walk down the aisle and become

Mrs. Dale Clayborn.

"Sorry about that. I got sidetracked, but I'm ready."

"So am I. I'll let you lead the way, Angel." Justina gave her a fake smile as the two ladies walked out while Supreme and Nico walked in.

"How lucky am I that I have two of the most handsome men walking me down the aisle." Aaliyah kissed both of them on the cheek. I'll never forget that you squashed your differences for one day so you could both be by my side."

"You know I would do anything for you, Aaliyah," Supreme said.

"So, would I," Nico agreed. "Now let's get this party started because you have an anxious groom waiting for you."

"Try not to make goo-goo eyes at Desmond when we're walking out," Angel remarked to Justina as the women took their positions.

"Give it up, would you, Angel."

"I know you're not denying it. I saw you and Desmond kissing by the glass doors."

"It's not what you think." Justina rolled her eyes, pissed she had to explain herself to a woman she didn't even like. "Desmond and I are in love. I haven't had a chance to tell Amir yet, but I will after the wedding. Are you satisfied! You can stop playing detective now."

"I have to give it to you, Justina, you are quite savvy. How you managed to convince an astute businessman like Desmond that you're worth the headache, has me stuck on stupid."

Before Justina had an opportunity to go in on Angel, the music began and it was time for the ceremony to begin.

Angel walked out first, leading the way. Justina was close behind and she could feel both Desmond and Amir staring at her. She wanted to make eye contact with Desmond, but thought it was too risky and Amir would notice. Justina had every intention of ending her relationship with Amir, but she didn't want to make things more complicated by throwing her relationship with Desmond in his face.

The minister, Dale, and the groomsmen were already positioned while Angel and Justina stood off to the left side waiting for Aaliyah to take her spot. The flower girl then came out throwing peach-colored rose petals that matched the dresses the women wore, for Aaliyah to walk on. The music for the bride to make her entrance started and the guests stood up anticipating her arrival. Aaliyah descended with Supreme on one side and Nico on the other. They walked down the stone path to the gazebo with waterfront views surrounded by lush Palm trees and manicured lawns. The Mediterranean décor mixed with tropical elegance was the perfect backdrop for the couple's nuptials.

Once the processional ended and the music faded off the minister asked, "Who gives this woman to be married to this man?"

Supreme and Nico said simultaneously, "We do." They let go of her arms, both hugged and kissed her, before giving Aaliyah's hand to Dale. Aaliyah handed her flowers to Justina so that her and Dale could hold hands and face each other.

The minister instructed everyone to be seated as he proceeded with the ceremony. After giving a short but meaningful script, the minister then addressed the bride to say her vows first.

"Dale, I remember the first day we met. I was my typical feisty self, yet you weren't overwhelmed. Instead, you allowed me to be me and we grew closer. Your willingness to embrace the good and bad in me made me adore and respect you even more. I never knew love could run so deep until I fell in love with you and because of that my life has forever changed. I promise to love you unconditionally, bring out the best in you the way you bring out the best in me. I look forward to us starting a family, celebrating our anniversaries, and growing old together as husband

and wife. You are my present and my future and I'm honored to be your wife."

Dale wiped away the tear coming down Aaliyah's face before the minister said it was his turn to say his vows.

"My beautiful, Aaliyah. When we met, I knew you had to be the woman for me. You were perfectly flawed. Looking at you was like seeing a reflection of myself. I had to make you my wife."

"That's so sweet." Aaliyah blushed.

"But then I realized I could never marry a woman like you. A woman that would stand in front of my face, look me in my eyes and lie to me over and over again. How could I ever call you my wife," Dale spit with disgust.

"Dale, what are you saying?" Aaliyah stuttered. She was overcome with confusion and fear.

"You knew your father killed my brother yet you lied, never said a word. He was the only family I had. You saw the pain I was in. Dying to know the truth, but the joke was on me."

"No! No! No! Dale, it wasn't like that."

"Then show me how good of a liar you really are. Look me in my eyes and tell me you didn't know your father killed Emory. Say it!" Dale barked.

Aaliyah felt as if the sky had fallen down on her. She thought her body was going to dissipate into dust. She felt like a nothing. Everyone seemed to be frozen due to shock. Justina and Angel wanted to comfort Aaliyah, but they couldn't move.

"Please, don't do this. I love you more than anything in this world."

"You did this!" Dale yelled as all the anger he had been containing burst through. "You and your family started this!" he continued to roar pointing his finger in Aaliyah's face. "But I'ma finish it." His voice then switched to eerie calmness.

All these men began standing up, one at a time, and they were armed. Even the groomsman standing next to Dale pulled out his gun. Then it clicked to Aaliyah. These were the same men she saw in Dale's office the day she left to stay at the hotel before their wedding. He had planned it all.

"Don't do this, Dale. Don't let our wedding day end like this," Aaliyah cried.

"Oh, I'm just gettin' started." He cut his eyes at Aaliyah. "Tell me. Who gon' die first?!" Dale scoffed, taking one of the guns from his man's hand and pointing it directly at Aaliyah's family.

Coming soon

Baller Bitches

THE REUNION

VOLUME 4

HOLLYWOOD

JOY DEJA KING

Chapter One

Nothing Seems To Be The Same

The gray skies filled with heavy clouds on the cold winter day satirized the grief looming in the air. The low rumble of distant thunder could be heard as guests arrived for the outdoor graveside funeral service.

"Do you think Blair and Kennedy are coming?" Diamond asked Cameron as they took their seats.

"Honestly..."

"Look," Diamond cut her husband off as she nodded her head towards the arriving cars. "It's

Kennedy. She came," Diamond said smiling. *Please God, let Blair show up too,* she prayed to herself.

As if the angels heard her pleas, a few minutes later a chauffeur-driven, black tinted Rolls Royce Phantom pulled up.

"Mommy, mommy, Auntie Blair is here!" Elijah exclaimed when she stepped out the car. "Do you think Donovan came?"

"I don't think so, sweetie." Diamond smiled, patting her son's head.

"I still can't believe she went back to that dude," Cameron shook his head and said as Blair and Skee Patron arrived hand in hand.

"All that matters is that she showed up... both of them," Diamond said, thrilled to see her best friends.

It had been a year since Diamond had spoken to Blair or Kennedy. Never did she imagine their reunion would take place at a funeral. Life had torn them apart, it seemed it took death to bring them back together.

P.O. Box 912
Collierville, TN 38027

www.joydejaking.com
www.twitter.com/joydejaking

A King Production

ORDER FORM

Name:

Address:

City/State:

Zip:

QUANTITY	TITLES	PRICE	TOTAL
	Bitch	$15.00	
	Bitch Reloaded	$15.00	
	The Bitch Is Back	$15.00	
	Queen Bitch	$15.00	
	Last Bitch Standing	$15.00	
	Superstar	$15.00	
	Ride Wit' Me	$12.00	
	Ride Wit' Me Part 2	$15.00	
	Stackin' Paper	$15.00	
	Trife Life To Lavish	$15.00	
	Trife Life To Lavish II	$15.00	
	Stackin' Paper II	$15.00	
	Rich or Famous	$15.00	
	Rich or Famous Part 2	$15.00	
	Rich or Famous Part 3	$15.00	
	Bitch A New Beginning	$15.00	
	Mafia Princess Part 1	$15.00	
	Mafia Princess Part 2	$15.00	
	Mafia Princess Part 3	$15.00	
	Mafia Princess Part 4	$15.00	
	Mafia Princess Part 5	$15.00	
	Boss Bitch	$15.00	
	Baller Bitches Vol. 1	$15.00	
	Baller Bitches Vol. 2	$15.00	
	Baller Bitches Vol. 3	$15.00	
	Bad Bitch	$15.00	
	Still The Baddest Bitch	$15.00	
	Power	$15.00	
	Power Part 2	$15.00	
	Drake	$15.00	
	Drake Part 2	$15.00	
	Female Hustler	$15.00	
	Female Hustler Part 2	$15.00	
	Female Hustler Part 3	$15.00	
	Female Hustler Part 4	$15.00	
	Princess Fever "Birthday Bash"	$9.99	
	Nico Carter The Men Of The Bitch Series	$15.00	
	Bitch The Beginning Of The End	$15.00	
	Supreme...Men Of The Bitch Series	$15.00	
	Bitch The Final Chapter	$15.00	
	Stackin' Paper III	$15.00	
	Men Of The Bitch Series And The Women Who Love Them	$15.00	
	Coke Like The 80s	$15.00	
	Baller Bitches The Reunion Vol. 4	$15.00	

Shipping/Handling (Via Priority Mail) $6.50 1-2 Books, $8.95 3-4 Books add $1.95 for ea. Additional book.

Total: $_____ FORMS OF ACCEPTED PAYMENTS: Certified or government issued checks and money Orders, all mail in orders take 5-7 Business days to be delivered